No Substitute

Susan Diane Johnson

No Substitute

Contact Information: titleadmin@pelicanbookgroup.com

All scripture quotations, unless otherwise indicated, are taken from the Holy Bible, New International Version[(R)] NIV[(R)] Copyright 1973, 1978, 1984 by Biblica, Inc.™ Used by permission of Zondervan. All rights reserved worldwide. www.zondervan.com

Cover Art by Nicola Martinez

White Rose Publishing, a division of Pelican Ventures, LLC
www.pelicanbookgroup.com PO Box 1738 *Aztec, NM * 87410

White Rose Publishing Circle and Rosebud logo is a trademark of Pelican Ventures, LLC

Publishing History
First White Rose Edition, 2012
Print Edition ISBN 978-1-61116-198-4
Electronic Edition ISBN 978-1-61116-197-7
Published in the United States of America

Dedication

To my son, Kirk, with all my love.

Special thanks and lots of love to my husband, Keith;
my parents, Bill and Barbara; and my sister, Pam, for
always supporting my dreams.

Praise for *No Substitute*

No Substitute is a tender, heartwarming story of lost love restored and is filled with the power of forgiveness. I loved it." ~ Sharon Gillenwater, author, *The Callahans of Texas* series

"Suzie Johnson has written a delightful debut romance novel. The book is full of entertaining twists and turns provided by the hero's playful teenage daughter. This story of love lost and rekindled is sure to warm your heart and inspire you to grow in grace and forgiveness." ~ Dina Sleiman, author, *Dance of the Dandelion*

"Be kind and compassionate to one another, forgiving each other, just as in Christ God forgave you."
Ephesians 4:32

1

"True or false, Miss Welsh? Did you ever date my father? Were you once in love with him?"

Amy Welsh squirmed in her chair at the front of the high school classroom, shocked by the unexpected question. Shayna Macmillan stared with unwavering blue eyes, and Amy wondered why on earth she'd ever agreed to be the subject of a mock interview.

The rest of Amy's students stared on in amusement. It was part of a class exercise, preparing her journalism students to do a real-life interview. Shayna asked to pose her questions to Amy rather than one of her fellow students. As Amy sat face-to-face with Shayna, it seemed as far as Shayna and the rest of the students were concerned, this interview was the real thing. The question appeared carefully chosen, deliberate, as if Shayna knew the answer but needed to hear it confirmed.

"He-llo-o, Miss Welsh." Shayna waved her hand in front of Amy's face, and a round of snickers drifted through the classroom.

"I—" Amy took a deep breath and glanced at the eager teenagers leaning forward in their desks with interest.

"Come on, Miss Welsh. Spill."

She wasn't sure which student spoke but it sounded suspiciously like Ashley Morgan, Shayna's best friend. They'd set her up.

"Yeah. Inquiring minds want to know." This, from one of the boys in the back row, set off a chorus of cheers accompanied by a couple of wolf-whistles.

"All right, people. This interview is over." Amy ignored their groans and stood, eager to get out of the hot seat.

"But Miss Welsh," Shayna protested. She jumped to her feet, her honey-blonde curls bouncing to one side. "We haven't finished yet." Hands on hips, eyes wide, her lips pressed together with determined insolence.

Amy blinked, surprised at the fierce resolve Shayna displayed. "*You* may not have finished. But *I* have. Besides, the bell is about to ring."

"I'd say this only lends credence to the fact you were once in love with my father." Shayna walked to her desk and collected her books with a huff.

Just then the bell sounded and the students—with the exception of Shayna—scrambled for the door.

Amy groaned. She should have known Shayna wouldn't let it go.

Since the day Amy took over this class two weeks ago, Shayna Macmillan proved to be most inquisitive. Without a doubt, she'd make a great investigative reporter someday—a young Diane Sawyer in the making. Smart, determined, and much too grown-up for her fourteen years, Shayna took advanced classes and would likely graduate a year or two ahead of the rest of her class.

Quentin must be extremely proud of his daughter.

An imaginary knife twisted in Amy's stomach whenever she thought of Quentin, and it never felt more real than now with his daughter standing before her.

Exactly where did Shayna learn about Amy and Quentin? And what compelled her to drag a confession out of Amy in front of the entire class? The girl definitely had a flair for the dramatic.

"I'm taking the fifth on this one, Shayna," Amy said. "Run along. You, too, Ashley." Shayna's willowy, redheaded friend lingered at the door, a suspicious twitch at the corners of her mouth.

"But Miss Welsh," Shayna said, "I just want to know—"

"Have a nice day, Shayna."

Shayna's eyes were unblinking, her stance determined. Amy ushered her toward the door.

Shayna stumbled toward it, dragging her feet in defiance, huffing in disgust. "Come on, just—"

"Keep it up, and you're looking at detention. Both of you." Amy looked pointedly at both girls before she firmly shut the door and leaned against it. Blessed quiet. The silence rang oddly in her ears.

Once again, as she had after her first day of filling in for Mrs. Baker, the English and journalism teacher who'd taken maternity leave, Amy questioned whether she wanted to be back here in the Washington town of Goose Bay. With her past laid out for her students to see, the questioning grew stronger. How on earth could Shayna have found out?

Certainly not from Quentin. She couldn't imagine him telling anyone about their past relationship. Especially not his daughter.

Not after what he did to me.

3

❧

"I'm home, Shayna." Quentin dropped his sports bag on the floor by the doorway, eager to hear about his daughter's day at school...especially journalism class. Even though he should be thinking about any number of problems at work, he'd thought of little else since Shayna brought up the name of her new teacher at the dinner table one evening. Today he left work early, and not even an hour of swimming laps at the local pool followed by a steamy session in the sauna could extract thoughts of Shayna's teacher from his overactive mind.

Miss Welsh. Could she possibly be *his* Amy Welsh? Amy Welsh with long silky brown hair and eyes as rich and dark as chocolate? He'd been hopelessly in love when they were teenagers. Could she really be back in Goose Bay after all these years?

No. Quentin shook his head and quickly dismissed the thought. Even if she was, she wasn't *his* Amy Welsh any longer. He walked through the living room, toward the kitchen.

"Shayna?" Silence met him. Puzzled, he furrowed his brow with concern. Why didn't she answer? His daughter always greeted him the minute he came home from work. In fact, he thought, sniffing the air, Shayna loved to cook and usually had dinner started. He didn't smell anything except the little cinnamon ornaments she'd baked last night. They were still spread out on the counter, waiting to be added to the growing pile of his daughter's craft projects.

As happened frequently, guilt pricked him. Playing lady of the house was too big a responsibility for a fourteen-year-old, even if she did seem to enjoy it. He never asked it of her after Karen died. Rather, his daughter seemed to naturally slip into the role. Perhaps it was her way of dealing with the loss of her mother. And while their neighbor kept her eye out for Shayna, it wasn't the same as having a woman in the house to talk to. Maybe he should hire a housekeeper, someone who would be company for a lonely teenaged girl. Although, with the way things were at work lately, he probably couldn't afford one.

Still wondering at Shayna's whereabouts, Quentin walked into the kitchen. Amidst the clutter on the table, a sheet of notebook paper caught his eye. His spirits lifted slightly and he smiled, touched by his daughter's sense of responsibility in leaving him a note.

Picking it up, he frowned. The scribbled note wasn't addressed to him. Quentin started to toss it aside, but two words caught his eye. *Miss Welsh.* A suspicious flutter teemed to life beneath his ribs. Unable to help himself, knowing he shouldn't, he quickly scanned the note.

You'll never believe this! Miss Welsh assigned all of us newbies to be partners with someone who took the class last year. You'll never guess who my partner is—Bradley Baxter! THE Bradley Baxter! DROOL!

Drool? His daughter was drooling over a boy? And the boy just happened to be Bradley Baxter, the very same boy he'd fired last summer when he'd caught him smoking on the job site and making sexist remarks to his female carpenter. Uh-uh. No way. Quentin clenched his fist, crumpling the note into a misshapen ball. He tossed it back on the table and began to pace the kitchen with heavy, hurried steps.

His daughter paired with that kid? Quentin shook his head, feeling his blood pressure rise. Not as long as Shayna was under the age of sixty-five. Baxter shouldn't even be in the same class as his daughter. Shayna skipped from seventh to ninth grade. But Baxter had to be at least a junior. Way too old for his little girl. Quentin stopped mid-step, glanced at his watch, and set his jaw.

School ended half an hour ago. The teachers should still be there grading papers or something. He and Miss Welsh were about to have a little talk.

Miss Welsh...Amy Welsh. No. *Miss* Welsh. He needed to think of her as Miss Welsh. Even if she turned out to be the Amy he'd known, as his daughter's teacher he needed to keep it professional. High school romances were long past, certainly not something to be rekindled after seventeen years.

Whoa! He must be lonelier than he thought to even be thinking along these lines. Could that be it? Loneliness? Or a matter of unfinished business between Amy and him?

Yes, Quentin assured himself. He didn't have an interest in rekindling anything. He merely wanted to fix the past. Settle things long left unsettled.

Besides, after the way their romance ended, there wasn't much chance of rekindling anything.

❧◈❧

Disturbed by her encounter with Shayna, Amy sat in her classroom long after she ordinarily would have gone home. When she came back to Goose Bay, she knew she wouldn't be able to avoid running into Quentin Macmillan—or even one of his children. Of course, she hadn't known for sure whether he actually had children, but given his sudden marriage to Karen seventeen years ago, he probably did.

But Amy hadn't expected it to be quite so painful, hadn't expected to take just one glance at a student and automatically know. One look in Shayna's dark blue eyes, and Amy had known the girl belonged to Quentin.

Picking up a piece of chalk, Amy began to scribble out tomorrow's assignments. Thoughts of Quentin and his ocean-colored eyes crept into her head, and she made one mistake after the other. She really needed to stop this. This very line of thought kept her emotions whirling into the wee hours each night.

Coming back here should have been easy. Amy hadn't made her decision lightly or without prayer. She prayed continuously when the job offer came and grew to believe God wanted her here in Goose Bay. The middle school in Issaquah where she'd worked for the last several years had trouble with state funding and cut several positions. Amy's job ended up as one of the casualties.

Teaching jobs were scarce this year, even in the nearby Seattle area. Out of work for months, Amy depleted her savings, and she'd been unsure what to do next. The Lord had obviously provided a job opportunity just when she'd needed it most.

Why then, was she overcome with these silly emotions?

Furiously scrubbing the eraser across the blackboard, she tried to dissipate the distracting memories. It didn't work.

Quentin Macmillan.

He filled her thoughts. She wanted to see him. She

didn't want to see him. Even though she hadn't seen him in years, she couldn't seem to forget him.

But I have to forget him. Every time I think of him, I sin.

The stray thought hit her like the tip of an arrow. Sharp, with a deep, barbed twinge. It wasn't the first time she'd thought it. She struggled with this very issue from the moment she first considered accepting the job.

"I'm sorry, Lord," she whispered. "I know he's married. Please forgive me. This is so wrong."

To emphasize the truthfulness of her thoughts, Amy slammed the eraser into the chalk tray and white powder flew everywhere. She rubbed her nose with the back of her hand.

Certainly she could deal with the past—put it behind her and go merrily on her way. Couldn't she?

Of course she could. She certainly hadn't mooned over him for the past seventeen years. OK, maybe she did at first. But once she came back to town and found out he'd married Karen, she put all thoughts of him out of her mind. At least she tried. It didn't happen overnight, but her heart healed eventually. She dated. Jared Parker even wanted to marry her. Amy pushed that thought away. She didn't want to think about Jared right now.

She just needed one glimpse of Quentin. One glimpse to prove he might have been the desire of her heart at age seventeen, but not now. Not at age thirty-four.

One glimpse, Lord, and I'll forget about him forever. One glimpse and I'll be able to get back to business— subbing for Mrs. Baker with the hope of a permanent job next fall.

But would she really?

Deep down Amy knew her thoughts were merely dictates of logic, in contrast with her heart's desire.

But my heart's desire is wrong. It's a sin.

Ashamed as she was, Amy still couldn't help hoping Quentin would walk in the door and instantly regret his broken promises.

I'm sorry, Lord. I trust You even though it doesn't seem like it. I know You've brought me here for a reason. Help deepen my faith and trust in You.

There. She'd prayed about it. She would be stronger now. God led her back to Goose Bay. She would be patient, trust Him, and wait to find out His purpose for her. *He* would strengthen her by wiping all thoughts of Quentin right out of her head and heart.

Could Quentin be her purpose?

Oh, Amy, you are so pathetic.

With a huge sigh, she closed her eyes and again apologized to the Lord. As ashamed as she was to admit it, she wanted nothing more than to spin around and open her eyes to find him standing there—the Quentin of her youth—waiting with open arms to sweep her away like his long ago promise.

How silly could she be? *Lord, please get him out of my thoughts.*

"Excuse me, Miss Welsh?"

Amy froze at the sound of the husky male voice. Did she really just spin around? A sick feeling rumbled in her stomach at the realization. Her arms were crossed around her waist, eyes closed like a fool, facing an unknown male. *Quentin?* Of course not. Thoughts don't conjure up people.

Then why was she so afraid to open her eyes?

Because if Quentin stood there, she'd have more

than momentary embarrassment to deal with; she'd also have to face the pain of the past.

Ever so slowly, Amy opened her eyes. As she did, her heart thudded and her breath caught in her throat.

Maybe thoughts really could conjure up people. Because there, with a storm raging in his eyes, stood her one-time heart's desire.

Amy's throat grew tight as her eyes focused solely on the man before her. Quentin's lips moved as he stepped toward her, but she couldn't hear his words. She'd dreamed of this moment countless times in the years since she'd left Goose Bay.

She'd also dreaded it—once again coming face to face with the boy she'd loved with all her heart. Man, she corrected herself, watching Quentin slowly walk toward her. He was most definitely not the teenager she remembered.

"Quentin." She sucked in a breath and hoped her voice didn't sound as shaky and breathless as it felt. Just saying his name caused her nerves to jitter.

In her dreams, she'd taken his youthful face and added to it. Fullness, maturity, laugh lines--all the things that came with the transition to adulthood. But she'd done it all wrong.

The man standing here was more rugged than the dream version of Quentin, more muscular. A stranger, if not for his eyes and mouth. Though fine lines fanned the corners of his eyes, and his mouth wasn't spread into the easy grin she remembered so well, she would have recognized him anywhere.

"I— uh—" She gaped at him a moment longer, her mind whirling.

His hair was still black as the night, thick, and, though cut short, still tried to work its way into a curl.

His shirt, the color of the Mediterranean, drew attention to his eyes.

The intensity Amy felt as she stared at him hit her like a sucker punch. The steadying breath she took was more a ragged wheeze. So much for attempting to regain her composure.

"Is there a problem with Shayna?"

What a stupid question. Why else would he be here? She bit back her disappointment and prayed for forgiveness...again. She would just keep reminding herself that Quentin had a wife and keep asking the Lord to scrub these thoughts from her mind.

"Amy, I— I can't believe it's really you. I wondered. Shayna keeps talking about Miss Welsh this and Miss Welsh that." One corner of his mouth lifted in a half-hearted, distant smile.

So he'd expected her to be here, discussed her with his daughter. This revelation startled her. It really could have been Quentin who'd told Shayna about their past.

Calm down, it doesn't mean anything. He's just a dad who came to see his daughter's teacher.

A *married* dad.

His face was weathered by years of hard work, sunshine, and laughter. Karen must make him very happy.

An awkward moment passed before Amy found her voice. "Yes, it's me." She laughed self-consciously.

"It's been a long time, Amy."

The smooth, honeyed tone of his voice made up for the warmth his smile lacked. And though she wanted to avoid it, she found herself looking into his eyes again. Amy tried to see past her painful memories but felt them blurring her vision.

"What are you doing in town? Besides the obvious, I mean."

"Someone wrote and told me about the temporary position. I always wanted to come back, so I thought I'd give it a try." She shrugged matter-of-factly and hoped she sounded nonchalant.

"You never married then?"

Blindsided by the question, Amy almost gasped out loud. Surely he didn't think every relationship she'd ever attempted had been overshadowed by thoughts of him? Or that she woke up late at night haunted by their unresolved past?

Undeniably defensive, she folded her arms across her chest. "So is this a social visit? Or did you come to talk about Shayna?"

Something flashed in his expression and then quickly disappeared.

"Actually, yes, I did come to talk about Shayna." His tone dropped in timbre. Amy recognized it as anger, and her stomach plummeted.

What could he possibly be angry about? Had Shayna told him about this afternoon? Even if she had, why would *he* be angry?

Amy neither confirmed nor denied Shayna's questions. More likely he thought Amy brought the whole thing up, which likely meant he wasn't the one who'd told Shayna about their former relationship.

"Shayna is one of my best students. Bright, eager, full of enthusiasm. Is she having a problem I'm not aware of?"

"She won't be having a problem once you take care of it."

Amy stiffened. His reply implied *she* was the one responsible.

"And what exactly is her problem?" She couldn't help lifting her chin a notch.

"Bradley Baxter." Quentin practically spat the name out.

"I don't understand." Amy frowned. A third-year journalism student, Bradley was one of her best students.

"You have Baxter paired up with my daughter. I don't want him within fifty feet of her."

"That'll be a bit difficult to manage in here." Amy glanced pointedly around the classroom.

"You know what I mean," Quentin said dryly. "The less contact Shayna has with him, the better. I don't want them working together."

Amy arched a brow and attempted to give him her best 'teacher's-in-charge' look, all the while ignoring the furious flutter of her heart. "Can you give me a good reason why not?"

"I have my reasons." Quentin folded his arms across his chest, as if to signal the end of the conversation.

But they weren't finished. Amy could tell by the set of Quentin's jaw he was holding something back. Something must have happened between Bradley and him in the past. Nothing else could explain his reaction.

"Quentin, without getting personal..." She flushed. Just saying his name out loud tied her tongue in knots. "I realize there's something you don't want to tell me and that's fine. But you have to understand I can't just go around changing the assignments mid-way through. Each couple is working on their interview questions. They—"

"Couple?" Quentin pulled at his shirt collar as if it

were suddenly too tight. "Understand this! My daughter is *not* going to be any part of a couple with that Baxter kid!"

Startled by his reaction, Amy took a step back. "Of course I don't mean 'couple' the way you just interpreted it," she said hurriedly. "I should have said each 'pair' of students."

"And my say-so alone isn't enough for you to change the assignments?" Now he sounded downright antagonistic.

Even though she didn't like it, Amy had to admit she did understand. He probably knew all the girls threw themselves at Bradley. Quentin was a daddy looking out for his daughter. She'd always wondered what he'd be like as a father. The thought tugged tenderly at her heart, and she hoped Karen cherished this protective "daddy" part of his nature.

A lump formed in her throat. "Think about it for a minute," she said. "I'm sure you know how girls this age are about things like this. You have to realize how humiliating this will be for Shayna."

"She'll get over it," Quentin snapped. Something flickered in his eyes. Uncertainty perhaps?

"Quentin, if I reassign Shayna, I'll need to give her a good explanation considering she's the one who asked to work wi—" She broke off suddenly, realizing what she'd been about to say. Too late, she couldn't recall the words.

"*She what?*" A bright red stain spread across Quentin's face, and the storm she'd noticed earlier in his eyes was back.

"P-Perhaps she doesn't know how you feel about him."

"Oh, she knows all right. He worked for me briefly

last summer, and let's just say it didn't work out. Shayna's heard enough of the details to know how upset I'd be over them working together. So I don't understand why she'd ask to work with him."

"Maybe she has a crush on him?"

Quentin pressed his lips together and closed his eyes. He took a deep breath then looked directly at her. The weariness on his face reflected in his voice when he spoke. "How can that be when she knows how I feel about him?"

Quentin rubbed his hand over his chin.

This turn-around tugged even harder at her heart. "There's no logic to the emotions of a girl's heart." The words swelled from deep within and pushed past Amy's lips in a whisper.

Taking one step closer, Amy placed a comforting hand on his upper arm. At least, she meant to be comforting. The instant she made physical contact, she wished she hadn't. Quentin's eyes widened. Hers probably did, too. She couldn't think about the firm muscular strength of his arms, how they'd felt wrapped tightly around her all those years ago.

Amy forced her thoughts back to Shayna, and Quentin's purpose for being here. "Does she date?"

"No, not yet," he whispered.

In that one sentence, Amy heard a loving father torn apart by the inevitability of his daughter someday putting him second.

"She's too young." Quentin glanced away.

Could he be thinking about their high school romance and how, even though they'd never done more than kiss, they'd been constantly inundated with the desire for a more mature relationship?

High up on the classroom wall, the clock ticked. Its

sound, suddenly loud in her ears, rivaled the pounding of her heart. Her hand went to her throat in a reflexive action.

Through the light blue threads of her sweater, she felt the single delicate pearl she always wore around her neck. Thankfully, the sweater kept it hidden from view. Quentin gave it to her the night he asked her to Homecoming—the dance she'd always dreamed of, but never did attend—and Amy didn't want him to know she still wore the necklace after all these years.

"Listen, Quentin, I..." She let her words trail away because his gaze now rested on her hand, which still touched his arm.

She'd meant it as a natural gesture, an attempt to comfort him. But he may well have misconstrued it. So much for keeping things professional. Instinctively she started to remove her hand, but he covered it with his own.

Warm, firm, tantalizing. The sensations filled her, teased her.

Lord, please forgive me!

Swallowing hard past the furious pounding of her heart, she looked at the floor. "Why don't I keep an eye on the situation? If it looks like a romance is developing, I'll give you a call."

"Sounds good, Amy. I'd appreciate it." The warm, honeyed tones were back.

Amy looked up then and saw him watching her closely. He smiled and she smiled back. He released her arm and headed for the door, leaving her emotions wrestling in a tumble of relief and disappointment.

He hesitated and turned back toward her.

"It's good to see you again, Amy."

"You, too, Quentin." She raised her hand in a half-hearted wave and instantly felt foolish.

The stinging sensation behind her eyes told her the truth with no uncertainty.

When Quentin walked through the door, a piece of her heart went with him.

Please, Lord, Jesus, help me. What am I going to do?

2

Quentin couldn't wipe the grin off his face as he left the school. He didn't have to wonder anymore. Amy was back. His Amy. For real.

Backing out of the parking lot, he felt like a teenager again. He recalled the many times he'd backed out of this same parking lot with her seated beside him, window down, a wide smile on her face, and her long hair flying free. Only this Amy was no longer a teenager. She'd matured, grown into a gorgeous, alluring woman, just as he'd always known she would. Though she was thinner than he remembered, she hadn't grown any taller. She was still five-two, the perfect height to fit in the crook of his arm.

OK, so he shouldn't be thinking this way. But he couldn't help it. Besides, he wanted to. He wanted to pinpoint exactly what made her look like a woman instead of a teenager.

Could it be the way she carried herself? Her poise, her self-assured manner of speaking? Instead of the first blush of teenage love, always so apparent on her face when they were kids, her face reflected a quiet confidence and a hint of mystery. A mystery he longed to discover.

Amy's short haircut surprised him, yet it suited her perfectly by accentuating the curvy planes of her face. It gave her a more womanly presence.

Things were finally looking up. In a burst of nostalgia, Quentin rolled his window down, turned up the volume on the "oldies" station, and roared down the street. Drumming one hand on the steering wheel, he sang along with Green Day's *Time of Your Life*.

રે⊸ન્ફ

Quentin returned home to find Shayna still gone. After looking all through the house, he stepped onto the back porch. "Shayna? Are you out here?"

"She ain't here, Mr. Macmillan."

Quentin turned to his left and spotted Mrs. Parsons, his elderly next-door neighbor, peering over her side of the fence. "Hello, Mrs. Parsons." He nodded to her and walked down the steps. "Have you seen her?"

"Sure have." Mrs. Parsons bobbed her silver-topped head enthusiastically, her cheeks flushed like two ripe apples. She always reminded Quentin of the grandmother he'd never had, even now with her mouth collapsed into a tight frown.

Uh-oh. Quentin groaned and prepared himself for the complaints to start.

"She's off chasing that duck of yours."

Rufus. Quentin rolled his eyes and stepped closer, bracing himself for the usual speech. She didn't disappoint him.

"Rufus quacks all day because he's lonely. And you should hear the ruckus he causes whenever the planes fly over."

Quentin sighed. Mrs. Parsons sounded rather like a quacking duck herself. He should be ashamed of himself for the wicked thought, but he wasn't.

Sorry, Lord.

"It's because he needs to be with other ducks, don't you know. I think it's cruel to keep barnyard animals as pets. And as for water, don't you know ducks prefer a lake or ocean to the plastic swimming pool you use as a duck pond?"

As she droned on, Quentin tuned out the familiar spiel. He rubbed his hand over his chin, then up through his short-cropped hair. He'd heard it all before and wouldn't waste his breath trying to give her answers.

Hens were the noisy ducks, not the drakes. He would admit Rufus probably quacked at the airplanes. Or when an eagle or hawk flew overhead. But all day long? No, he simply didn't believe her.

As for being lonely, he'd tried giving Rufus to a buddy who lived out in the country. Nick had a pond full of ducks and geese, but it didn't make any difference. Nick claimed Rufus pined away, lonely for Quentin and Shayna. He wouldn't eat with the other ducks, wouldn't swim with the other ducks, and finished dead last in the pecking order. After a week Nick called and told Quentin to come and get his homesick pet. He and Shayna gladly went and retrieved Rufus.

Everyone had been happy since. Everyone, that is, except Mrs. Parsons. She rested her plump arms atop the cedar fence, her chin propped on the back of her hands.

Quentin winced, thinking about itchy cedar splinters and the tiny welts they caused. But the thought vanished when he heard the rest of Mrs. P.'s lecture.

"Furthermore, I've done some checking. Do you

know there's a city ordinance against keeping farm animals in town?"

Were ducks considered farm animals? Horses he could understand. But ducks? He pulled his shoulders back and tried to pay closer attention.

He'd lived in this house all his life, except during his stint in the military and had ducks since he was a small boy. No one ever bothered to complain, let alone point out a city ordinance. The mayor lived right down the street and didn't seem to see anything wrong with it. Sometimes he even came and fed Rufus his leftover lettuce leaves. Surely he wouldn't do that if it were against city codes. No, Mrs. P. was probably just angry about Rufus nearly scalping her cat the other day.

"I'm telling you, Mr. Mac, you'd better do something about your duck or I will."

Quentin blew out a heavy breath, hoping she was merely being a bored busybody. He'd have to do some checking though, in order to be sure. He'd been taught to respect the law. He taught Shayna the same thing, tried to teach her a sense of responsibility and how to make the right choices. How could he expect her to distinguish right from wrong if he couldn't do the same?

He wished he could walk away from his neighbor and pretend she'd never said a word about it. But she had. And it would break Shayna's heart if Mrs. P. spoke the truth.

"Oh, by the way..." Mrs. P.'s smug tone stopped him in his tracks. "Wait 'til you get a gander at your daughter." She pressed her lips together, clearly waiting for his response. Sometimes—times like this—Mrs. P. could be very exasperating. Annoying, really.

"Get a gander? What do you mean?"

"Then you really don't know?" The corners of her mouth twitched, and a gleam of amusement brightened her watery blue eyes. The same look she always donned whenever she had something she felt was her absolute duty to report.

"What's she done this time?" He sighed and stepped closer to the fence. At times, his daughter could be equally as exasperating as his neighbor.

"Oh, nothing for you to worry about," she said quickly. "But you're not gonna like it, not one bit."

"What?" He closed his eyes briefly, annoyed with himself for practically biting off the elderly woman's head. Still, he checked the urge to apologize. An apology would only feed her delight.

"She cut her hair."

For a moment Quentin wasn't sure he'd heard her right. How could Shayna have cut her hair? She'd had long hair since she was a toddler.

Mrs. P. made a scissoring motion with her fingers. "It's gone," she said matter-of-factly. "All that beautiful honey-colored hair." She paused, waiting for a response. But, at a momentary loss for words, Quentin couldn't offer one.

His neighbor made a clicking sound with her tongue and cheek then sighed regretfully. "Well, I've gotta get in and stir my beef stew. You know how grumpy Foster can get."

"Yes." For once Quentin didn't feel like laughing at her reference to her battle-scarred tomcat.

After a smile and a quick wave, she disappeared beyond the fence leaving Quentin feeling alone and confused. He didn't mind if Shayna cut her hair. It was her hair, after all. As long as she didn't do anything strange like shave it down the middle, he could deal with it. No, it bothered him because she'd never said a word about it.

His daughter was growing up, he realized as he trudged back toward the house. The days where she discussed everything with him were quickly ending. Smart and independent, of course Shayna would move away from being daddy's little girl. It was only natural. He didn't like it, but he'd have to accept it.

Unsure how to feel about all of this, Quentin went back into the kitchen. He hadn't been there five minutes when the back door burst open and Shayna staggered in. She leaned against the frame with an exaggerated stance and let her chin fall to her chest.

"So?" Quentin smiled at his daughter's dramatics. "Does this mean you caught Rufus?"

"Yeah." Shayna lifted her head and gave him a quirky half-smile. And Quentin felt as if the wind had been knocked out of him. Her once long wavy hair now fell in soft curls and framed her face in a gentle halo of dark blonde wisps.

"Do you like it?" She looked down again, this time appearing shy.

He nodded and tried to speak past the painful lump in his throat. "You look..." *Stunning, beautiful, too classy for the likes of Bradley Baxter.* "...just like your mother." Truthfully, she did. Never had Shayna looked more like Karen than now with the short tendrils framing her face, highlighting the angles of her cheekbones.

"Thanks." She looked up at him again, a hint of moisture in her eyes.

"She would have been so pleased." Tightness squeezed his chest, even though Karen had been gone three years.

"I thought I needed a change. In case you were wondering why I cut it."

Quentin could only nod. She didn't have to explain. He knew. She wanted to impress a boy. And impress him, she would. Baxter would go crazy over her. Who wouldn't? She looked more mature, one step closer to womanhood. He needed to stop this situation before it had a chance to get started.

Don't even think about it, he wanted to say. He knew how devastating teenage love could be. His daughter wouldn't fall in love with Baxter. Not so long as he had a breath left in his body. He wanted to spare her the inevitable heartbreak a kid like Baxter would bring.

"So," Shayna said brightly. "We traveled around the neighborhood twice before Rufus took a wrong turn and ended up between Mrs. P.'s fence and the corner of her house."

"Oh, great." Stunned by the change in his daughter, Quentin realized he'd forgotten all about Rufus and Mrs. Parsons.

He could well imagine the duck trapped between the fence and the house, quacking loudly and beating his wings while Shayna tried to pick him up. Without a doubt, the disturbance had to be the perfect topper to his earlier conversation with his neighbor.

"Yeah, old Parsnip wasn't too happy about it."

"Shayna." Quentin tipped his head and speared her with a level stare. "How many times have I asked you not to call her that?" It might have been cute when Shayna was younger, but now her voice held a hint of disdain instead of affection. "You're old enough to know better."

"Well, she just makes me mad."

Frustrated by his daughter's defiance, Quentin huffed under his breath and turned away. He tried to teach her respect, honestly he did. But lately it seemed all his efforts were for naught. His exuberant daughter challenged him at every turn. He turned back to her. "Try to remember to have a little respect for Mrs. P., even if you don't always agree with her. OK?"

"I never agree with her. She's a fruit-bag."

"Shayna." Quentin lowered his voice in warning. "Knock it off or you'll end up grounded."

"Oh, all right." Shayna slapped her arms across her chest and wrinkled her nose. "But I don't know what your problem is. It's not like she can hear me or anything."

"That is hardly the point. You should always be respectful. It's not something you can turn on and off, you know."

Shayna turned away from him, and Quentin had no doubt she was rolling her eyes or pulling some weird face to declare her feelings for what she no doubt viewed as an incompetent adult. He'd caught her doing it before. She turned to face him again, her smile sincere. "Sure, Daddy."

Quentin reached out and embraced his daughter. Resting his face against the top of her head, he knew he'd never grow tired of holding her this way. He prayed she, in turn, would never grow tired of hugging her dad.

"So," he said when Shayna finally squirmed away. "Whaddya say we go out for pizza?"

"Alfredo's?"

"Hmm, I don't know," Quentin teased. He didn't want her to know she had him wrapped around her finger. "They're always so crowded and noisy."

"Please? They have the best cheesy garlic bread, and this is Tuesday. You know what that means? Free root beer!"

Free root beer. Quentin loved it when Shayna dropped her guard and let her youthful enthusiasm shine through.

"Well," he said slowly, unable to keep a grin from sliding across his face. "Since you exerted so much energy chasing after Rufus, I suppose Alfredo's it is."

"Great!" Shayna gave him another hug before racing him to the door. "Let's go now 'cause I'm starved."

Quentin deliberately put aside thoughts of journalism class, Baxter, and the new haircut. He planned to enjoy the evening with his daughter.

But some thoughts were difficult to push aside...like those of Amy and the youthful way she still made his heart pound.

❧

Amy needed to stay as far away from Quentin Macmillan as possible. In fact, as her rowdy students burst into the classroom the next morning, she thought maybe it would be better if she just left Goose Bay when school let out for the summer.

Originally she'd planned to stay through the summer. It would have given her enough time to deal with her feelings toward Quentin and decide if she should pursue a relationship with Jared Parker.

Now she wondered if she should just go back to Issaquah. Then she would only have eight weeks left here. Eight weeks to try to avoid running into Quentin again. Eight weeks to try to forget Shayna Macmillan, student extraordinaire, was Quentin's daughter. His and Karen's.

Pressing the backs of her hands to her cheeks, she felt relieved to find them dry. It wouldn't do to have the students asking questions. Especially her most inquisitive student—Shayna Macmillan.

She forgot to ask Quentin if he told Shayna about their past. She forgot to ask him about Karen. She forgot a lot of things in that instant when he'd placed his hand over hers.

Oh, who was she kidding? She'd forgotten merely because she'd been in his presence again, all the while fighting valiantly to keep her emotions at bay. Especially the one of betrayal. She didn't want to think about it, didn't want to feel it. Thankfully she'd been able to keep any sign of her inner turbulence from him.

During class, Amy followed through on her promise to keep an eye on Shayna. There was nothing unusual in the girl's actions, and she certainly didn't seem to be obsessed with Bradley, though she couldn't say the same for Bradley.

From the first day Amy stepped into this classroom, she'd noticed Bradley's crush on Shayna. But up until she'd asked to work with him, Shayna seemed a bit cool toward him. Even today, she seemed more interested in passing notes to Ashley and receiving comments and compliments on her new haircut.

After class, Shayna and Ashley were the last ones to leave. Amy observed them out of the corner of her eye as she gathered up her assignment book and tote bag. They giggled and whispered, and it almost seemed as if they wanted to be noticed. Ridiculous.

Her conversation with Quentin caused her to be

suspicious. She pressed her lips together, irritated at him, irritated at being dragged to the level of spying on her students.

"Have a good evening, girls." Amy reached over to flick off the lights.

"You too, Miss Welsh." Ashley giggled, which garnered her a poke in the ribs from Shayna.

"Be quiet," Shayna whispered loud enough for Amy to hear. "You're going to..." Ashley shut the door behind them, drowning out the rest of Shayna's sentence.

Most curious. Amy pushed the door open, hoping to hear some more of this conversation. But the two girls were huddled just outside the classroom, their heads bent together, obviously in no hurry to leave the building. Amy had no choice but to continue walking, slowly, in hopes they would eventually draw near enough for her to hear them. Each step left her feeling like the lowest sort of eavesdropper, and she couldn't believe she'd allowed herself to be dragged into this. Where was her professionalism, her sense of dignity?

Sweeping her irritation aside when she sensed their sneaker-soft footsteps behind her, she strained to hear their conversation. Snatches of whispered words drifted to her, but no complete sentences. The words *boys, sister's car, drive-in,* and *spending the night* sent a wave of alarm through her. If she hadn't believed Quentin yesterday, she certainly did now. The girls were definitely up to something.

Amy thought of Quentin's desire to keep his daughter from falling for the wrong boy. Should she tell him? If Shayna ended up with a broken heart, she'd never forgive herself.

Unable to help herself, Amy glanced over her

shoulder. The two girls came to a halt in front of a row of lockers.

What now? She couldn't hear a thing. Amy bit her lip uncertainly, then, in a moment of inspiration, unclipped her pen from the cover of her assignment book and let it roll to the floor in the direction of the lockers.

Pleased when the pen headed in Shayna's direction, Amy slowly followed it. Looking down, she tried to tune back in to the conversation. A well-worn sneaker stopped the pen before it could roll under the lockers. She swallowed a groan before looking up, recognizing the sneaker.

Stewart Snyder. Photography teacher. Poster boy for the nerd society, right down to the masking tape on the nosepiece of his black glasses. As always, Amy's heart went out to him. Desperate for a date, he always seemed to wear his heart on his sleeve and continually hounded Amy no matter how many times she said no. Now he stood to ruin her chances of determining what the impulsive teenagers were up to.

"Whew, that was close." Stewart's husky voice didn't seem to match anything about him. He stooped down and grabbed the pen, then held it out to her. "Here you go, Amy." As she took it, his sweaty hand brushed against hers. She resisted the urge to wipe it on her skirt.

"Thank you, Stewart." She tried to smile at him but feared her ire showed through anyway, irritation at Quentin for making her stoop so low as to spy on her students. But then, he'd always had that effect on her. A smile, a lift of the eyebrows, a touch on the arm... She'd always been, and obviously still was, too much like putty where Quentin was concerned.

"I didn't want it to roll under the lockers," Stewart said. "It might be lost forever under there, and I thought, I don't know, it might be special or something."

"No, it's nothing special." This time, Amy gave him a genuine smile. Stewart was so sweet. She sincerely hoped some woman would recognize it someday. It just wouldn't be her.

A locker door slammed shut.

"Just a dime-store pen," she said in a rush. "But thanks just the same." She looked away from his hopeful stare, wondering how to leave without seeming too abrupt. But when she looked away from Stewart, she noticed someone had joined the girls at their locker. Bradley Baxter. He gazed down at Shayna, a curious expression on his face.

"How do you know this will work?"

"Because." Shayna's tone sounded unfriendly, almost harsh, and Bradley flinched. "You know my dad can't stand y—" She broke off suddenly and glanced around, her gaze sweeping across the hall where Amy stood with Stewart. Turning back to her friends, she said loudly, "This is going to be so cool. I can't wait 'til tomorrow night."

Alarmed, Amy turned and headed for the office. "Excuse me, Stewart," she said over her shoulder. "I have to go."

She needed to look up Quentin and Karen's phone number and let them know right away. The girls really were planning on going to the drive-in movie with boys. Bradley Baxter included.

Granted Bradley seemed nice, but she wasn't Shayna's mother. Her parents had the right to know about their plans. But did they really? Didn't teenagers have the right to make their own mistakes and learn from them?

But what if those mistakes could be prevented?

"Hey, Amy, I wanted to—" Stewart's voice was cut off as the office door closed behind her. Amy felt a pang of guilt. She resisted the urge to open the door and apologize. It would only encourage him.

After retrieving Shayna's file from the school secretary, Amy punched in the phone number. While the phone rang, her focus strayed to Shayna's statistics. She pulled her gaze away, knowing she didn't have a right to look at it for anything other than a phone number. But before she could scold herself further, she'd scanned the page.

One glaring absence stood fresh in her mind. Karen. Karen Macmillan wasn't listed anywhere on the stat sheet.

Were they divorced? The girl Quentin married immediately upon high school graduation was no longer in his life, and Amy thoroughly disliked the twinge of gladness she felt upon the realization.

Ugly thoughts, Amy, ugly thoughts.

She asked God to remove those thoughts from her heart. She'd been praying about the hurt and bitterness for years and thought she'd dealt with them fairly well until she came back to town and they slammed her full in the face again. *Lord, Jesus, I can't do it without Your help and guidance.*

"Macmillan here." Quentin's deep voice startled Amy out of her thoughts.

"Quentin, hi. It's Amy."

"Amy. I didn't expect to hear from you."

Did that mean he was glad? Or did it mean she was intruding?

"I, um, need to talk to you about Shayna and her plans for tomorrow night." Unsure how to take his comment, Amy stumbled over her words.

3

He would ground Shayna for life!

Quentin paced the living room, stopping every few feet to glare at the telephone. Amy frustrated him almost as much as his daughter. After stating the purpose for the call, she'd simply hung up. She hadn't bothered to discuss the situation with him or offer any advice. Wasn't she supposed to be the expert on teenage girls?

So what should he do now? She'd said the girls were planning to sneak out of Ashley's house tomorrow night and go to the drive-in with Baxter and some other boys. Not if he could help it.

Determined, he headed up the stairs.

This was his fault. Raising a teenage daughter grew more difficult by the day, and somehow he'd failed. Shayna needed a woman to talk to and he'd never thought to provide one.

Pausing outside the door of Shayna's room, where she'd disappeared as soon as the dinner dishes were done, he wondered what he should say. Theoretically, the words should come easily to him. They'd always had a warm, open relationship.

Until now.

Until Shayna decided to start lying and sneaking around.

He'd tell her she couldn't stay the night at Ashley's.

Without another second's hesitation, he rapped on her door.

"Shayna?" He opened the door and stuck his head in the room. She sat on the bed staring absently at a poster on her wall—some smart-alecky kid from a TV show. She was probably mooning over Baxter though, not really seeing the kid on the poster at all.

"Shayna," he said again.

"Hmm?" Shayna looked over at him. "Oh. Hi, Dad."

Did she seem disappointed to see him? Or did he just imagine it?

"Do you want to play a game of Monopoly or Battleship?"

Rolling her eyes in disgust, she shook her head. "I'm busy."

Busy? Doing what? Staring at the wall?

"OK then. If you change your mind—"

"I won't," she interrupted.

Confused, hurt, Quentin didn't know what to say. All of a sudden he'd been relegated to a bothersome adult his daughter no longer wanted to spend time with. This was so unlike Shayna, so unlike their way of relating to each other, he was at a loss over what to do. To bring up the slumber party and her plans now would undoubtedly result in an argument. An argument he didn't feel like having at the moment. They would, however, discuss it thoroughly before she went to Ashley's tomorrow night.

If he let her go at all.

Quentin quietly shut the door. "I'm at a loss, Lord," he muttered. "Help me to understand this."

Walking down the hall toward his own room, thinking about Shayna drooling over a no-good kid,

Quentin clenched his jaw in disgust. That his daughter would become interested in boys was bound to happen someday. He just didn't understand why it had to be now, and why it had to be Baxter.

He flipped on the light and groaned at the sight of a week's worth of laundry piled on his bed waiting to be folded. Switching on the radio, he clenched his jaw harder as the voice of Dr. Wendy Wakefield filled the room. He couldn't stand that woman. She thought she knew everything about everything, claimed she was a good listener. Ha. He'd heard her many a time when she hadn't truly listened to the caller. He thought radio psychologists were the biggest blight on the American public since cell phones and text messaging bombarded their way into everyday life.

Absently, Quentin picked through the pile of laundry searching for towels to fold. He liked to fold them first. It gave him a sense of accomplishment to see them stacked in neat piles.

Dr. Wendy's first caller shared her problems with her thirteen-year-old son. The second caller complained of some problems with a co-worker. Thus far, this evening, Wacky Wendy seemed at the height of compassion. And her advice wasn't half bad either.

No. Absolutely not. Ridiculous. He didn't need advice on raising his daughter. Still, it might be good to get an outside opinion on whether or not Shayna should be grounded for life. No. It was crazy.

Perhaps he could blame it on the fear of losing his daughter to a no-account kid with a bad reputation. Perhaps it was the certainty that he'd failed to meet the needs of his teenaged daughter who desperately needed a mother. Quentin wasn't entirely certain why but, feeling more ridiculous than nervous, he reached for the phone.

He'd only get a busy signal. What were the chances he'd even get through?

Surprised when the call connected, he almost dropped it.

"This is Stan at Ask Dr. Wendy. Do you have a question for her?"

Quentin coughed and tried to remind himself of why he'd dialed the phone in the first place.

For Shayna.

"Hello, are you there?"

"Uh, yes. Sorry," Quentin muttered. "I have a problem with my daughter. She's uh—I just wanted to know if I should ground her or how exactly I should handle it." Great. He sounded like intelligence in all its glory. What a stupid idea. He felt like a jerk.

"What's your name?" asked Stan in his disinterested voice.

"Qu— John. John." OK, so John was his middle name. Hopefully that didn't count as a lie, but he couldn't risk giving out his first name.

"OK, John." Stan didn't sound convinced of the name. "There are a couple of callers ahead of you. Stay on the line and when Dr. Wendy comes on, ask your question as clearly as possible. She'll want to know how old you are, how old your daughter is, if you're married, that sort of thing. Oh, and make sure your radio is turned off."

Stan placed Quentin on hold, though instead of dead air he could hear the radio through the phone. He reached over and switched his radio off, sat on the bed, and wondered exactly what he was doing.

The guys at work would sure make this rough on him if they had any inkling. He quickly dismissed the thought. What were the chances of them listening to the good doctor anyway? Most likely they were camped in front of the tube with a pizza, all set to watch nightly reruns.

He listened as Dr. Wendy raked some poor caller over the coals. She'd gone from sympathetic to self-righteous in the space of two seconds. Not a good sign.

"John, are you there?" Stan's voice came across the line. "You're next. Remember, no need to be nervous. State your statistics followed by the question. Dr. Wendy will be right with you."

Before he could answer, he heard the irritating nasal voice of Dr. Wendy say, "Our next caller is John. Welcome John. How may I help you tonight?"

"Uh, ye— It's my daughter. She's fourteen—"

"How old are you John?"

"Thirty-four."

"Married or single?"

"Single. Widowed." Was all of this necessary? *Just let me get some help for Shayna, Lord. I need to know what to do for her.*

"So, John. What exactly is the problem with your daughter?"

"She likes this boy. I found this note—"

"You *found* a note? What do you mean you *found* a note? Were you snooping through her things?"

"No, it was on the table with her notebook and—"

"You looked through your daughter's notebook? John, haven't you ever heard of a little thing called privacy?"

"It was on the—"

"Privacy John. Privacy."

Oh great. Just exactly what he needed. A lecture instead of advice. What had he been thinking?

Quentin clenched the receiver, torn between defending himself to this wacko and hanging up on her. Everyone he knew was probably listening, and by tomorrow morning it would be all over town.

≈∞

Amy sipped a cup of tea and flipped through her class papers while she listened to Dr. Wendy Wakefield. The radio psychologist didn't always say things Amy agreed with, but the show was fun to listen to while she finished grading school papers.

She knew the poor guy Dr. Wendy was giving a hard time to was Quentin. There was no mistaking his husky voice. It certainly had deepened with age, and caused shivers of awareness to trip up her spine. She couldn't help but laugh at the name he'd chosen.

At first she'd been shocked to hear his voice come over the radio. What possessed him to call a radio psychologist? And since when did he take advice anyway? A lot must have changed in the last seventeen years.

"Now you've got your daughter's teacher in on it, too?" Dr. Wendy sounded incensed. "John, John, John." She tsked. "You've taken the entire trust issue and turned it upside down. Your poor daughter. I cannot believe...."

Growing more and more outraged as Dr. Wendy went off on her usual diatribe, Amy hung on her every word. Quentin was a good father looking out for his daughter's welfare. It was entirely possible his personality had changed over the years, but she really didn't think he was the overbearing and controlling type. And even though he'd asked her to keep an eye on Shayna, Amy knew it wasn't because he wanted to snoop for the purpose of invading her privacy. He wanted to keep his daughter safe. Was there anything wrong with that? Breath held, Amy waited for his response. When none came she pictured him on the end of the line, eyes closed, head bent, in agony over this dilemma with his daughter and the way this woman twisted it around to belittle him. He must be humiliated. Either that or he was livid.

Amy straightened the stack of homework papers from her fourth period English class and set them in her briefcase. The phone rang as she reached for another stack of assignments. Distracted, waiting for Quentin to answer Dr. Wendy, she mumbled into the phone without thinking.

"Hello?"

"Amy?"

She recognized the voice immediately.

"Quentin." She paused. "I mean, John."

He met her teasing with dead silence.

"Sorry," she mumbled.

"So you were listening."

"Yeah, still am as a matter of fact. I guess you hung up on her."

"I did." He sounded proud of the fact.

"Well, it might interest you to know she's still lecturing you on the values of privacy and trust. None of your business, John, none of your business."

"I should have known better than to call Dr. Wacko."

Amy laughed. "Actually, I'm not surprised at the way she treated you. I listen to her a lot, and there are a lot of people who are probably sorry they ever called her."

"Listen, Amy." His voice lost the teasing edge, and Amy's heartbeat sped up. "I hope you don't mind me calling you."

"No, not at all." She was annoyed at how happy hearing his voice made her feel.

"I wanted to talk to you about Shayna."

Why did that not surprise her? She struggled to keep the disappointment from her tone. "Look, Quentin, I—"

"No, Amy. Hear me out. I'm not trying to talk you into separating her from Baxter again. I just want some help. You seem to know more about girls this age than I do. What should I do?"

"I don't really know all that much, Quentin, other than the fact that I was once her age."

"Yeah. I remember."

At the husky intimacy of his voice, her stomach plunged and her pulse quickened. Good thing they were on the phone rather than face-to-face. She'd hate for him to see how he affected her.

"So, you want to know whether or not you should lock her in her room until she's forty-five?"

"Something like that, yes."

"I honestly don't know, Quentin." She sighed heavily. "I think to tell her she can't see Bradley would be a huge mistake. I mean, think about when you were her age. If your parents told you that you couldn't see someone, wouldn't it make you want it all that much more?"

"Yeah," he said. "If I remember right, that's exactly what happened."

Her stomach took a dip again. She swallowed hard. "Bad...or good...example. Depending on how you want to look at it. What about her friends? If you tell her she can't go to the slumber party, what do you think will happen?"

"She'll be angry at me. Sulk. Stick her bottom lip out and wrap me around her finger."

Amy couldn't help smiling to herself. "Yes, Quentin, but kids get angry at their parents all the time. I mean, she'll want to know why. I'm not saying you have to give her an answer. You could be like other parents and say 'because I say so.' But she's in high school now. Much as you may not like it, it's a fact. And she's smart. There won't be much you can say in your defense to keep her home. It won't take long before she knows the reason. And you know what you'll do?"

"Push her right into his slimy grip," Quentin finished.

Amy blinked and pushed the hair out of her eyes. "I wouldn't have put it quite that way, but yes. You will."

"So do I just ignore her plans to sneak off to the drive-in and meet this little drool machine?"

Amy laughed. "No, you don't ignore it. We just need to think this through some more."

"I always loved that about you, Amy. Thinking everything through before you make a decision. Some things never change."

Loved? It was a figure of speech, nothing more. He probably didn't even realize he'd said it.

"I— I need to go now, Quentin."

"May I call you tomorrow then? For advice, I mean?"

Advice? Again, a prick of disappointment. She nodded, then realized he couldn't see her. "Yes. School's out at two."

"Great. I usually take my break then. I'll pick you up at the school, and we can go get a burger."

He was moving way too fast for comfort. "Quentin—"

"And we'll talk," he said quickly. "Nothing more. About Shayna. I talk better with a cheeseburger in front of me."

Amy sighed when she finally hung up. A burger with Quentin to talk about his daughter? It wasn't supposed to be this way. She'd seen him, talked to him. She should be able to forget about him now. Go on her way. Think about starting a deeper relationship with Jared. Jared, in Issaquah, patiently waiting for an answer to his proposal. Jared who understood she needed to think things through before she could commit.

Guilt pricked her at the thought of Jared. Before she left Issaquah, they talked on the phone daily. Other than letting him know she'd arrived in Goose Bay, she hadn't called him. She really needed to, but she just couldn't make herself do it tonight. Amy sighed. Texting would be so much easier, but it wasn't something they usually did, and to start now would most likely give him the indication she didn't want to talk to him. The thought struck her right in the middle of her conscience. Could that be the truth?

In spite of Jared, and knowing what she should do, Amy couldn't help her feelings of anticipation at seeing Quentin tomorrow.

And part of her was panic-stricken.

The last time Quentin said he'd meet her someplace, he hadn't showed. She couldn't bear it if he stood her up again.

෬෬

"You're certainly in a good mood this morning, Dad."

Quentin came to a stop at the bottom of the stairs he'd taken two at a time, and stared at his daughter. His good mood faded faster than a ten o'clock sunset. She stood smiling at him, her head tilted to one side. Her new shorter curls brushed artfully against one cheek.

Guilt assailed him. He'd been thinking about Amy, looking forward to their lunch together, not concentrating on what brought them together in the first place—his daughter and her plans for tonight.

His daughter should have been the one dominating his thoughts, along with a plan to keep her away from Baxter. Instead he'd been thinking of Amy. She'd been back in his life one day and already his priorities were quickly spinning out of whack.

"Good morning, sugar." He planted a kiss on top of her head and then forced himself to smile even though his guts felt all twisted. "If I seem happy, it's because I've got the most beautiful, grown-up looking daughter in the world." He mussed her bangs and said, "This new haircut sure does suit you."

Shayna gave him a sparkling smile, and he knew that even if he didn't want his daughter looking too grown-up, his words of praise made her feel wonderful.

"I made your favorite breakfast."

"Let me guess. Cinnamon-brown-sugar toaster pastries?"

Her smile grew wider, and she turned toward the kitchen.

Wondering how best to approach her, he followed. Directly? Subtly? Forcefully?

"Shayna." He reached for one of the warm pastries piled on the plate she placed in front of him and broke it in half. "About your plans for tonight..."

It might have been his imagination, but he was almost positive Shayna's hand trembled as she reached for her juice. Guilt over lying to him? Or excitement over her plans?

"Oh yeah," Shayna said brightly—too brightly, in his estimation. "Ashley's mom is renting some really great DVDs for us to watch. *Pride and Prejudice* and *Emma.* I know we've seen them lots of times, but they're both so awesome. And she's going to make us some popcorn. Real stuff, not the microwave kind, with lots of salt and butter, and..."

As Shayna rattled off her plans, Quentin was struck by a painful observation. His daughter was an accomplished liar. It slammed him like a fist to his solar plexus then squeezed his heart. When had it happened? It hurt that his daughter, with whom he'd always had a relationship of honesty and respect, could and would lie so smoothly.

He fought the urge to jump up and shout, "You're lying, and I forbid you to ever see Bradley Baxter again." Instead, he bit off a hunk of pastry that was decidedly lacking in brown sugar and cinnamon. It stuck in his mouth like a dried-up blob of flour.

He could say nothing about Shayna's lying, or her plans. Nothing at all. Not yet. Amy said it would be best not to forbid her to go. It would only make matters worse. He needed a strategy, and Amy would help him figure one out this afternoon. So there, he told himself. He didn't need to feel guilty about Amy dominating his thoughts. She was there for a purpose. To help keep Shayna safe from Baxter.

Feeling better after coming to this conclusion, Quentin reached for his juice, took a long swallow and changed the subject.

"Is Rufus safely locked in his pen?"

Shayna nodded. "Safe and sound, and hopefully he'll remain that way."

"Good. Because the last thing I want to do when I come home tonight is chase down a transient duck." Or deal with Mrs. P. He'd have to remember to make a few calls today to check into her claims.

"It'll be fine, Dad. I'm more worried about dinner. Should I come home before I go to Ashley's and make you something to eat?"

She was too young to be worrying about such things. He really had to try and find a housekeeper he could afford. Maybe someone who could be a sort of mother figure. This really wasn't fair to Shayna.

Quentin leaned over and kissed the worried look off his daughter's face. "You worry too much, sweetheart. I'll miss eating with you, but I'm a grown man and perfectly capable of taking care of myself for one night. You have a good time, and don't worry about me."

He nearly choked on those last words. Hopefully, though, he and Amy would come up with something to keep her plans from ever happening, to prevent her from having the kind of good time he knew the Baxter kid wanted.

4

As soon as Quentin pulled up in front of his office building, his stomach knotted. Shayna and Amy had successfully swept work problems from his mind. But now he had to face them again.

His business was in trouble. Every time he bid on a construction project, he was outbid. And by the same company, too. He had a feeling it was an inside job. It certainly appeared as though someone was feeding bid information to the competition.

The thought of one of his employees—most of them friends—stabbing him in the back... Quentin shook his head. He couldn't comprehend it. And yet, for the last few weeks he'd looked at each one of them with suspicion. He didn't like the way it churned his guts.

Trying not to think of the problems awaiting him, Quentin locked his truck and headed across the graveled parking lot.

"Well, look who's here. If it isn't *John*." Bobby Farrell, one of the finish-carpenters, greeted him as he stepped through the entryway.

Great. Just great. The laughter and snickers that followed Bobby's greeting could only mean one thing. One, or *all*, of them had heard the radio show. It was the last thing he'd have expected from a bunch of construction workers. His secretary maybe, but not the rest of the crew. Of course, he'd learned long ago not to second-guess any of them. He took a deep breath and blew it out hard before looking at his employees. Each one of them wore a grin that needed to be knocked right off their faces.

All except Russell Miller, his project manager and good friend. Russ stood a little apart from the others. His eyes were lined with tension, and his grin seemed to be forced. Something was very wrong in Russ's life. This wasn't the first time Quentin sensed it. He needed to make some time for the two of them to talk.

Quentin first noticed the change in his friend a few weeks ago, and it seemed to only grow worse. He felt a pang of guilt. He'd been so busy thinking of Amy, he'd all but ignored one of his closest friends.

"Hello-o. Quentin?" Louise, his secretary, waved a hand in front of his face.

Everyone stared at him. Waiting for an explanation, no doubt. Yeah, right. Like that would happen.

"Don't you guys have work to do?" Quentin scowled at them, quelling the urge to slap them all upside the head. Then he glanced through the glass window of his tiny office. Puzzled, he frowned and leaned closer, studying the room. His desk was missing.

"Where is it?" he demanded.

"You're in a particularly lousy mood this morning," Russ commented. In spite of the teasing tone is his friend's voice, Quentin heard the underlying tension. Yes, they definitely needed to talk. But now wasn't the time. He couldn't spare any sympathy toward Russ in front of the other guys, or Russ would never live it down.

"Yeah, I am. And I'd like to stay that way. Now

where's my desk?"

As if he didn't have enough on his mind already. Amy, Shayna, the wandering duck, the humiliating radio show, Russ, and now this. And he had work to do—a business to try to save. Sick and tired of their practical jokes, he did a quick scan of the outer office and glared at each employee.

"Don't make me ask again."

Bobby, the apparent ringleader, shrugged nonchalantly and walked away. "I don't know what you're talking about."

Quentin looked at Louise who refused to make eye contact, though he did detect a smirk playing around her pencil-lined lips. They thought they were all so funny. He didn't see the humor in it, but he didn't have time to argue either. He'd save the arguing for later.

"I don't have time to play games. Get out of here, all of you." He had to finish the supply list for the cabinets at the bakery and then work on his bid for the new bank. He grumbled under his breath and walked through the open door of his office.

Apparently his staff had a modicum of respect for him because his paperwork sat on the floor—right where his desk should be. Grumbling some more, he grabbed the papers pertaining to the bakery and plopped himself on the floor—where his chair should be. But settling down to work was no easy task because thoughts of Amy and their upcoming lunch kept crowding his mind.

❧❧

Amy didn't know how she'd get through the day.

She sat at the desk in her empty classroom, staring at the clock, watching the second hand slowly click around the face, marking each second with a tick. Earlier that morning she'd considered calling in sick. Though it would have been close to the truth, she couldn't bring herself to do it. The school might not be able to find someone to substitute on short notice, and she hated to dump anything on anyone at the last minute unless it was an emergency. Besides, sitting at home wallowing in apprehension over meeting with Quentin wouldn't do her any good. She was better off here, at school.

She swallowed hard past the swelling lump in her throat and blinked hard. *Do not dwell on the past.* The thought, a Scripture from Isaiah, whispered through her and she acknowledged, grudgingly, that yes, the past was over and done with and it served no point to dwell on it. Who could change it? Only God. *If* He cared to. An instant of guilt pricked her heart. No, she wasn't being fair. Quentin made his decision seventeen years ago, not God.

The first bell rang and two dozen kids burst through the door and slid into their seats, reminding her that she needed to concentrate on teaching. It wasn't until later, during her break in the teachers' lounge, when she allowed herself to think about her meeting with Quentin. She refused to call it lunch.

Lunch sounded too much like a date, and a date with Quentin was the last thing her heart could take. Besides, she thought as she dipped a teabag into her mug of hot water, she intended to eat during her regular lunch break. Not with Quentin. If she waited until two o'clock, when school was out, she'd starve.

"You look like you lost your only friend."

Amy looked up and smiled half-heartedly as Miki approached her from across the room.

Miki Loretta was a tiny woman, delicate and ultra-feminine, an unusual and lovely mixture of Japanese and Italian. She was also kind and generous in spirit, with a delightful sense of humor. Her dark, slightly tilted eyes twinkled as she sat down across from Amy. "Since I thought that honor fell to *moi*, I know it's not true. Unless..." Miki paused dramatically and raised one eyebrow. "...there's something you haven't told me."

Amy couldn't help but grin. Miki was a great drama coach, but she would have been even better in the spotlight.

"You don't want to know." Amy tried to sound nonchalant, but when Miki looked at her with those piercing dark eyes, she knew she'd failed.

"Relax, Amy. Things will change. I promise. Before long, you'll get to know lots of people. I just heard some of the other staff members say how lovely they think you are."

"Might one of them have been Stewart Snyder?"

"Come on," Miki coaxed. "It can't be as bad as you think."

If she only knew. Amy had never shared her secret heartbreak over Quentin. Though Miki had been her friend in school, probably the closest thing she'd had to a best friend, they hadn't really kept in touch. Their friendship had only recently been rekindled, and it didn't go deep enough yet for her to share her deepest hopes and hurts. Since Miki was her friend in school, she knew Amy and Quentin had dated, she just never knew how it all ended.

"I'm having a little trouble with one of my

students. No," she amended. "It's actually the parent."

"Let me guess. Mom swears up and down that her precious son would *never* put dyed rabbit pellets in your M&Ms jar."

Amy had to laugh at Miki's imagination. "Something like that."

"Don't sweat it." Miki gave her a gentle pat on the shoulder. "These sorts of problems occur all year long. Every parent thinks their darling can do no wrong. At least that's what they say. I'll bet deep down each and every one of them knows exactly what their beloved teenagers are capable of."

"I think that's the problem," she said cynically. "This parent is afraid to admit his kid might be human." Not wanting to explain further, Amy made her excuses and prepared to get back to her classroom.

"Wait," Miki called out before she could disappear through the door. "We're having a potluck after church on Sunday. Why don't you come?"

"I'll think about it." Amy shut the door behind her, hating to disappoint her friend but reluctant to commit. Truthfully, she'd yet to attend church since coming back to Goose Bay. Not because she didn't want to. It was just so hard to walk into an unfamiliar church for the first time—even if she did know at least one person there. She missed the fellowship, longed for it in fact, and knew she'd have to make an extra effort to take that first step.

More than once during her afternoon journalism class, Amy had the sensation of being watched. A couple of times, she'd glanced up from her desk in time to see Shayna quickly look away. Did she suspect Amy had overheard the girls' conversation yesterday and worry her dad might find out? Good. Let her worry. Maybe she'd think twice about sneaking out of the house tonight.

Any hopes Amy had of Shayna changing her mind were dashed as soon as class was over. As Shayna and Ashley were leaving the room, she heard the word 'drool' several times followed by titters and giggles. Though she'd been worried before, Amy now knew she'd made the right choice in mentioning Shayna's plans to Quentin. She glanced at the clock. Now that her last class was over, she had a forty-five minute planning session before meeting him. Would he show up?

Amy's stomach knotted with apprehension. She shut the door behind the last of the classroom stragglers and slowly walked toward her desk.

Forty-five minutes could be a long time. Forty-five minutes to sit and think...to wonder and worry.

About Quentin.

Would he stand her up again?

❧❦

"Louise, contact..." Quentin glanced at his watch. One-forty-five. He had just enough time to get to the school and meet Amy. He dropped the folder on his secretary's desk and ignored her raised brow. "Look, you take care of this. I have to go."

It hadn't been easy working without a desk, but once he'd put thoughts of Amy to rest, the morning had practically flown by. All he'd had to do was put those brown eyes out of his mind and stop thinking about the way her chestnut hair brushed her delicate jaw line, forget how it had felt as she'd touched his arm, and how tender and warm her hand had felt beneath his own.

Everyone seemed to stop work and stare at him as he headed to the men's room to wash up before leaving the office. He'd been so busy he hadn't been in there once today. He swung the door open and stopped with a groan. He should have known. There, for all to stumble over as they walked in or out, sat his desk. His chair sat on top like a throne, and toilet tissue was strung over both. He turned to glare at his laughing employees, who stood scattered throughout the office staring as if they'd waited all day for this moment.

"I don't even want to know," he said with disgust.

"Maybe you should call Dr. Wendy," Bobby said. Then, pointedly and in a false voice, "John."

Everyone burst out laughing, and Quentin felt the corners of his mouth twitch—until he looked at Russ, who once again hung back from the crowd looking lonelier than he'd ever seen him.

Before he could think about it further, Louise added, "I'm sure she'll give you some good advice on dealing with ornery co-workers."

"You're not my co-workers. You're my employees." He growled with frustration. "And I know exactly how to deal with you. Or, how I *should* deal with you. But I don't have time right now. I'm late for an appointment. I expect this desk to be back in my office when I return. And no more of your stupid pranks. That's not what I pay you for."

"A date?" Louise asked immediately interested.

"Why would you say that?" Was it that obvious he had a woman on his mind?

"You usually eat in the office. I noticed you didn't even bring your lunch today."

He shrugged innocently. "I didn't get to the grocery store yet. Now will you people kindly mind your own business and get back to work? *After*," he added meaningfully, "you get my desk back where it belongs."

ॐॐ

At ten after two, Quentin hadn't arrived. Amy felt like a fool, sitting on the bench under the trees lining the parking lot. Of course, she should have expected this. It's only exactly what he'd done to her before. Promised he'd be there and then not shown up.

She should have just told him she'd meet him somewhere else. Sitting on this bench was an ironic twist of fate. It was the exact bench she'd sat on in a wind and rainstorm on a dark November night nearly seventeen years ago.

She'd huddled there, two bags holding her most precious belongings, soaking up the rain and mud, trying not to feel the cold as she waited for Quentin to pick her up in his battered blue truck. But it wasn't until he was an hour late that she'd even felt the need to huddle and try to block out the cold, since she'd been so flushed with excitement over this new adventure with him.

Because her father was in the military, her family moved a lot. Her father's new orders were taking her family halfway across the world to Germany, and from Quentin. She'd been heartbroken at the prospect of leaving him. But he'd brilliantly, and romantically, come up with the idea of running off to California where they would get married. They'd both cleaned out their respective savings accounts earlier that day.

Between them, they had barely enough gas and food money to get to California. But they weren't worried. Jobs were supposedly plentiful in the Golden State. Besides, they had each other. That was all that mattered.

Quentin had wanted to leave right then, but Amy had insisted she go home and have one last meal with her family. She'd say good-bye in her own way, leave them a note, then sneak out. Just before she'd gone in the house, Quentin had gently touched the single precious pearl she wore around her neck. The one he'd given her a few short weeks ago. Then he kissed her and whispered a promise that he'd love her forever. She was his and he was hers...for keeps.

It hadn't been easy saying her silent good-byes to her family over the dinner table, then writing the note she'd hoped would explain all her heartfelt love for them. But she also loved Quentin, and the thought of never seeing him again hurt worse than any pain she could imagine.

That was before he didn't show up...before her heart shattered into tiny bits.

Two hours after Quentin was supposed to show up, Amy had forced herself off the bench and slowly trudged home through the dark, muddy woods behind the school.

Once in the house, she'd retrieved the note and despondently added her bags to the pile of luggage already sitting at the front door. At seven in the morning her family—Amy included—would drive to SeaTac Airport and board a plane that would fly them out of the country.

All the rest of the night she sat in the darkened living room, waiting, hoping Quentin would call or come by. But he never did.

Pride kept her from calling him. Silly, stupid pride. Because she knew with a certainty that sometime after he'd dropped her off at her house that afternoon, with a kiss and a promise to pick her up in the school parking lot at ten, he'd stopped loving her.

If her parents or sister thought there was anything strange about the mud on her baggage the next morning, or her disheveled clothes and hair, they never said a word.

As they drove out of town, Amy leaned her forehead against the car window and watched Goose Bay fade in the distance. What didn't fade though were the memories of Quentin kissing her tenderly, passionately, telling her he loved her for always and that they'd be together forever.

And as it had the night before, her heart shattered all over again as she realized her dreams for a future with Quentin would never happen. She'd wanted to jerk the pearl necklace from her throat, but for some reason she'd stopped herself. It was almost as if by doing so she'd tear all traces of Quentin from her memory, and she hadn't quite been ready for such a huge step.

Now, all these years later, she was startled to realize just how painful those memories still were. Even more surprising was the moisture on her cheeks, the blurring of her eyes. Fumbling in her purse, she was dismayed to find no tissue. She wiped her eyes on the sleeves of her pale yellow sweater, thankful she didn't wear eye make-up. Then she looked around. Still no sign of Quentin. History was repeating itself. She just must be the kind of woman men stood up.

A sick dejected feeling started deep in her stomach

and Amy stood, ready to leave. At the same moment, she heard the sound of an engine in the distance. Her heart picked up speed as a vehicle, a pick-up truck, came into view. Quentin? The honking of the horn confirmed her hopes. She was so relieved, her knees almost gave out as she walked toward his truck.

Not old and battered and blue like the one he'd had as a teen, this one was black and shiny and new with *Macmillan Construction* professionally painted on the side panels. So he was in construction. She wondered what happened to his dream of being a wildlife photographer.

Quentin left the truck idling as he jumped out in a rush. He wore a red flannel shirt and black jeans, and his blue eyes were shadowed with concern. "I'm sorry I'm late, Amy. I had some things to deal with."

By his disgusted tone, she gathered he wasn't happy with something at work. "Problems?"

"No. Not any longer. Come on. I'll tell you about it on the way." He hurried around to the passenger side to hold the door for her. Amy smiled, remembering that the Quentin of her past was nothing if not a gentleman. She was glad he hadn't lost that touch.

Amy settled comfortably into the plush passenger seat of Quentin's truck, noting it appeared to be first class all the way. No hard bench seats in this truck. It was a far cry from the old beat up one he used to drive. She snapped her seatbelt into place then turned to Quentin with her nose wrinkled up.

"What?"

"It smells a lot better in here than your old truck used to."

He burst out laughing, which injected a sense of ease into the air and gave Amy the courage to finally ask if he'd been the one to tell Shayna about their past.

"No." He seemed genuinely surprised, so Amy had no reason to doubt his denial.

"But who did, and why?"

Keeping his eyes on the road, Quentin shook his head. "I don't have the slightest idea. How do you know she knows?"

Briefly, Amy filled him in on the day in class where they'd done the mock interview.

After hearing all the details, Quentin glanced at Amy for a brief second before looking back at the road. "I'll bet it was Ashley's mom. She likes to keep the pot stirring. All the time." Amy couldn't help laughing, but she was still puzzled. "How would Ashley's mom have known about us, and why would she tell Shayna?"

"Ashley's mom is Misty Morgan."

The name meant nothing to Amy. She shrugged. "So?"

"Misty Morgan used to be Misty Conner." After a moment's pause, he added, "One of Karen's close friends in high school." Quentin didn't even glance at Amy; he just kept his eyes glued to the road.

"Oh." She didn't want to talk about Karen, even if Quentin did. Feeling the sudden tension in the air, Amy changed the subject as smoothly as she possibly could, even though her insides quaked. "So, tell me. What happened at work this morning to make you so tense?"

Amy listened with amusement as Quentin detailed the morning's escapade with his employees. Truth to tell, she could just picture his irritation with his staff. By the set of his jaw and the light dancing in his eyes, she knew it was irritation mixed with fondness. He must have an easy relationship with them. Otherwise they would have known to draw the line at hiding his desk in the men's room. She liked this little glimpse into his working relationships.

"So why did they do it? I mean, practical jokes I can see, but why the desk? And why hide it in the restroom?"

"I think it was the only hiding place they could find. If I'm reading them right, it was their way of telling me my life is in the toilet."

"Your life?" Amy felt dumb even asking.

Instead of answering, Quentin cast a sidelong glance at her, his lips pressed together.

"Oh." Understanding dawned. "They heard the radio show."

He nodded. "I think they lost some of their respect for me today."

"How can that be? Everyone has problems."

"Yeah but not everyone calls wacky talk-radio shrinks."

That was true, but it seemed to her he'd done it in a moment of desperation. Who could blame him for that? "I think it shows how much you care."

"They think it shows how incompetent I am."

Something was definitely wrong in Quentin's life, but he obviously didn't want to share it with her.

"Quentin, you're far from incompetent. You're a wonderful, caring father, and you're a good provider. No one can point a finger at you and say you haven't given Shayna everything you possibly can."

"Everything except a mother."

Karen. Quentin was missing his wife. She ached to reach toward him, to take his pain away.

"She's fourteen years old. You can't just pick a

woman to replace her mother. She's old enough to know you'd just be doing it for her sake. She's smart enough to realize it wouldn't be for the right reasons."

"You're exactly right. But I'm afraid Russ doesn't see it that way."

"Russ?"

"Russell Miller. My project manager. He's also a good friend of mine. I think you'd remember him if you saw him."

Amy nodded, even though she wasn't sure she remembered a Russell from high school. "What does he have to do with whether or not you call a talk-radio show?"

Quentin sighed. "Russ would call it looking out for my best interests. I call it interfering in my life. To put it bluntly, he's always looking for a reason why his sister needs a husband and why I need a wife."

"So by going on the talk-radio show you've given him more ammunition for his argument."

"Yes. And I'm sick and tired of hearing the argument."

"Is she pretty?" Amy regretted the question as soon as it flew past her lips.

"Not as pretty as you."

An uncomfortable silence settled in the truck as Quentin kept his eyes on the road and Amy resisted the urge to turn away. If she did that, he'd know how his words had affected her. Instead, she merely glanced down at her lap.

Pretty. Did he mean it? She'd always wanted to be pretty, and had always hoped Quentin found her as such. Obviously he hadn't since he dumped her at the first chance and then married Karen.

Beautiful Karen, cheerleader, long blonde hair

styled just like Jennifer Aniston from *Friends*—Amy still enjoyed watching the reruns—with perfect white teeth and her skin always tanned to perfection. The girls outside of Karen's popularity group always had a running joke that she used a tube of mascara a week and sunbathed whenever the sun peeked through—no matter that there was only one month a year in Goose Bay when it was warm enough to sunbathe.

Though Karen and Quentin had been best friends since they were young children, Quentin always assured Amy they were friends and nothing more. Still, Amy always felt inadequate and rather like an ugly duckling whenever Karen was around.

At the moment though, Amy felt nothing but mean. Here she was thinking hateful thoughts about a woman who was no longer alive. As soon as Quentin pulled up in front of the diner, she hopped out of the truck and headed for the door, relieved to be able to turn her thoughts to something besides their troublesome past—though she wasn't entirely sure Quentin's problems with Shayna were less than troublesome.

Help me, Father, she prayed. *Help me help him. And help me understand why I've found myself in this situation.*

Heart pounding, Amy led the way into the restaurant and wondered about God's plan in all of this.

5

When Quentin dipped his last fry in ketchup, Amy said, "I haven't been able to come up with a solution for you."

For some reason, they'd avoided talking about the purpose for their lunch. Almost as if talking about it would take away something from the very fact that they were together again. No, not *together*, Quentin reminded himself. Just a little problem solving. Instead, he'd entertained her with the antics of his employees.

Now, pressing his lips together, he nodded. "I understand. It's hard to say 'do this or do that,' when it's not your kid."

"Quentin, it's not that! Really. I thought about it all night. Honest I did." She used her straw to twirl the ice in her tea then picked up the straw wrapper and began folding it into neat little squares.

"I know." He sighed wearily. He'd noticed the circles under her eyes earlier when he picked her up. At first he thought maybe she'd been crying, but she'd blamed it on hay fever. "I thought of nothing else, myself." *Liar.* But he couldn't very well tell Amy he'd spent most of the night thinking of her instead of his daughter. He was no better than the predatory teenager he was trying to protect Shayna from. "I, however, was able to come up with a solution."

She dropped the paper she'd been fiddling with

and gazed at him. "You have?"

"Yes." His heart thudded uncharacteristically as he prepared himself for her reaction. "You can help me keep an eye on her."

"Oh, Quentin, I thought I'd already agreed to that." Amy looked away from him and stabbed her straw at the lemon in her iced tea. "While she's in my class and if I see her in the halls and notice anything—"

"No, I don't mean like that. I mean, tonight, while she's at the drive-in. You can go there with me, and we can keep an eye on her and that Baxter kid. And if he so much as puts one layer of epidermis on her, I'll—"

"Wait just a minute here. What are you talking about?" Amy stared at him incredulously and he squirmed under her gaze.

Don't let her say no. Quentin hadn't realized until that moment just how much he wanted her to say yes. And not just to help keep an eye on Shayna.

"I'm not going to the drive-in with you."

Disappointed, he let out the breath he'd been holding. "Amy, please—"

"Forget it."

"But Amy, you don't understand—"

"Yes, I do. You, Quentin, are the one who doesn't understand. I'm Shayna's teacher. It would be—" She picked up the straw wrapper again, twisted it a few times before it broke, then glanced around the restaurant as if she could snatch the right words out of the air. "It would be unprofessional. And I'm not going to the drive-in with you to spy on her." She dropped the remnants of the paper into her glass, stood, and headed for the exit.

Disappointment crushed Quentin as he hurriedly pulled out his wallet and dropped some bills on the table. Then, hoping he could catch up and reason with her, he left the diner hot on Amy's heels.

ॐॐ

Amy couldn't believe Quentin wanted her to go to the drive-in with him. That was the last place she wanted to go. Memories of the past were bound to surface there, memories she didn't want to relive. She was supposed to be putting him out of her mind, forgetting about him.

Now that she'd seen him again, she realized the further you got from the past, the bigger and brighter it seemed. Quentin had been so built up in her mind, all other men paled in comparison. But the reality was, Quentin was a man just like any other. A man, plain and simple. Why then, did she have this fantasy that he would whisk her away on a white horse and make all the pain of the past disappear with the sunset?

Halfway down the sidewalk, she froze when someone caught her by the arm. She knew it was Quentin before he even spoke. She knew because his touch sent a pang of longing right through her. *Don't turn around*, her common sense warned her. *Don't look into his eyes.* Blue eyes. Eyes she'd fallen in love with at age sixteen. Eyes that had crept into her thoughts more than once over the years.

"Don't leave." His deep voice vibrated straight to her heart. "Please?"

Unable to help herself she turned around, but refused to make eye contact. Instead, she concentrated on the red flannel shirt that accented his muscular build. She noticed the third button from the top was missing. Perhaps she should offer to sew it back on.

"What do you want me to do?" She fought to keep the weariness from her voice.

"Just come to the movie with me. We can keep an eye on Shayna. That's it. Just help me protect my little girl."

His pleading tore at her heart, and she looked up without thinking. Immediately, she wished she hadn't. He studied her with his intense gaze, blue the color of the Pacific on a sunny day, and she felt the breath woosh from her lungs. She wanted to turn away, go back to studying the buttons on his shirt, but it was as if she were a puppet on strings with the puppeteer forcing her head up.

"I know you want Shayna to be safe. I understand that, and I want to help. But Quentin, she's not a little girl anymore. She's fourteen. To a girl, that's almost a woman."

Quentin looked as though she'd shot him through the heart, and that look had her feeling as if she'd been shot as well.

"I'm sorry," she whispered thickly. "I know it's not easy watching your daughter grow up."

"It's not. Sometimes I wish I could turn back the clock and keep her four years old forever..."

...*with a mother.* Amy finished his unspoken words silently. Her heart felt heavy. Why, oh why, had he married Karen? Was that why he'd stood her up? Had Karen been prettier? Kissed better? What had she done wrong? The questions that had haunted her for the last seventeen years continued to haunt her now as she observed that faraway look in Quentin's eyes. She knew without a doubt he was thinking of Karen.

The loneliness he must be feeling tore at her, and she wished she could do something, anything to ease his pain. Maybe that's why she was here. To help him through this crisis with his daughter. Maybe that was why God was throwing her together with Quentin when she'd been trying so hard to put him out of her mind. God *wanted* her to help Quentin. And if that meant going to the drive-in movie, that's what she'd have to do.

"So," she said with a brightness she didn't feel. "What movie will we be seeing?"

❧

Clothes littered the bed and the light blue carpeting beneath. Unsure whether to opt for the 'teacher' look, or to go casual, Amy had changed half a dozen times. Dressy was definitely out, since they were just going to the drive-in movie. Not that it should matter what she wore. It wasn't like she hoped Quentin would notice her.

Or was it? Her heart thudded.

Though she didn't like to admit it, she'd had a few sleepless nights over the years that inundated her with thoughts of him. But never more frequently than after she'd made the decision to come to Goose Bay. Those thoughts were becoming so intrusive they might actually drive her insane. That, in fact, was part of the reason she'd come here.

Every single relationship she'd ever had was over before it began because she compared every man to Quentin. Of course, she wasn't really comparing them to him. Rather, she'd built him up in her mind to be someone larger than life even though she didn't really know him anymore. And how much had she really known him then, anyway? They'd been teenagers, kids. They hadn't even known who they were, let alone known each other.

That's why she had to deal with this and put it behind her. So she could get on with her life and maybe even have a love life. Maybe even with Jared. Jared, a highly respected Seattle lawyer, was the first reliable man she'd ever dated. He was caring, compassionate, attentive, and never let her down.

Still, every time he tried to hold her hand or kiss her, memories of Quentin besieged her.

So when Amy had received a Christmas card from Miki mentioning the temp job, she'd jumped at it. Ever patient and supportive, Jared was quite understanding about her decision. But he also let her know in no uncertain terms, that he'd be waiting for her when she decided to return.

As soon as she'd arrived in town, knowing it was a matter of time before she'd run into Quentin, Amy began a fervent prayer campaign. *Please let me talk to him one time. One more time, and I'll be able to get him out of my system forever.* And she'd never doubted God would answer her prayer. But she didn't understand the way He answered. Why was she being thrown together with Quentin in this quest to 'save' Shayna from her behavior?

Had the Lord seen into the deepest recesses of her heart, known what she'd barely dared admit to herself? That what she'd secretly hoped for all along was not only to see Quentin again but also to spend time with him? Maybe, she reasoned as she rummaged through skirts, sweaters, and jeans, maybe she needed more than a passing glimpse to get him out of her mind. Maybe she needed to spend time with him for the actual healing to begin. Maybe helping Shayna was just an added bonus.

Then, when the school year was over, she could go back to Issaquah and marry Jared. Something about that thought didn't sit well with Amy, but her cell phone chirped at her before she could think it through. Her first thought was that Quentin was calling to cancel. But then she looked at the name on the screen.

Jared.

Coincidence? Amy didn't think so and considered not answering. She meant to call him when she thought about it the other day, but she still hadn't. He'd be hurt.

Not allowing herself time to think about it, Amy flipped open the phone. "Jared, hi."

"Amy?" Instead of his usual warmth, his voice resonated with a clipped, icy tone. She'd been right, he was hurt.

"Jared, I'm sorry it's been so long since I've called you. It's just that there's been this thing with one of my students and…I don't know. That's not a very good excuse for ignoring you."

"It's OK. I understand." His voice warmed just a bit. "I know you've been busy getting settled into your classroom and your rental home. But other than calling to tell me you made it there safely, I haven't heard from you. Amy, I miss you."

The plaintive edge to his last comment tugged at Amy's heart and she started to answer back. But a flash of awareness struck her and she realized she'd be lying.

Lying? Really? Amy sighed. In truth, she missed his friendship and their conversations, but she didn't miss him. She closed her eyes and tried to picture him, but the image was faded, blurred, not sharp and clear like when she thought about Quentin.

"Jared, I really do feel bad that I haven't called you sooner. And I feel even worse because I can't talk right now. I have someone picking me up in a few minutes, and I'm not ready. But I'll call you tomorrow afternoon, if that's OK."

"Are you going on a date, Amy? With *him?*" The clipped tone was back.

"No, Jared, I'm not going on a date. But I am going with Quentin, if that's who you're referring to." She was hurting him, and she hated it. "I said I'd help him with his daughter. It's too hard to explain right now. I'll tell you about it tomorrow when I call." She looked at the clock. "I really hate to do this, but I do need to go. I'm sorry."

This time it was Jared who sighed. "I am, too, Amy. Good night."

Amy said good night, but when he didn't answer, she realized he'd disconnected and most likely hadn't heard her. Feeling like a rotten excuse for a human being, Amy blew out a heavy breath and turned back to the closet. Her heart was no longer into picking just the right thing, and she really needed to get ready.

Relaxed was best. She finally chose her favorite blue jeans and a sweater. An old-fashioned looking sweater with cabbage roses was feminine yet warm and comfortable. She always did get cold at the drive-in, and something told her she'd better not count on Quentin to warm her up like he had in the past. Nor should she even be thinking along those lines.

By the time she was dressed, she'd managed to exchange the heaviness her heart felt over hurting Jared for a case of good old-fashioned nerves. She realized it when her hands trembled as she buttoned her sweater. That's why her thoughts were so rambly and nonsensical.

She really should to turn it over to God. He knew her deepest thoughts. But her deepest thoughts and desires didn't necessarily equate with what was best for her, and He only wanted what was in her best interest. She should stop trying to second guess Him, stop trying to rationalize things. She needed to stop fighting it and let God take care of things--to trust Him more.

As she smoothed down the fine lace collar of her sweater, Amy's finger caught in the chain at her neck. For a brief moment, she froze. The necklace. She couldn't wear it. Even if she tucked it into the sweater as she always wore it, the shape of the collar would allow it to be seen. She didn't want Quentin to know that after all these years she still wore it. She removed the necklace with regret and placed it on her dresser, then sat down to put on her shoes.

After lacing up her sneakers, Amy glanced in the mirror for a final inspection then back at the necklace that glittered against the doily on her dresser. She brought her hand to her neck, surprised at the empty feeling she found there. Sighing deeply, she left the room, determined to leave these bereft feelings behind.

There were more important things to concentrate on right now, like her nerves and how she was going to get through tonight with Quentin.

It wasn't a date, she reminded herself sternly. Not a date. Just a mission. To protect Quentin's daughter.

చ౮

"What are we going to say if Shayna sees us?"

Amy's voice had a nervous edge to it, which echoed the churning emotions in the pit of Quentin's stomach.

"We'll just tell her we're on a date." He kept his tone deliberately matter-of-fact, never taking his eyes off the road. If he so much as glanced at her, she'd be able to tell with only the illumination of the dash lights and passing cars just how much he wanted that to be true.

A date.

The truth was, until he'd driven up to find her waiting for him on the white-washed porch of her little yellow country house, the porch light casting a shimmer on her chestnut brown hair, he'd done a fairly good job of convincing himself this was merely a means to an end. A way to keep his daughter safe.

But Shayna aside, he wanted it to be more. If only there wasn't a past standing between them. A past he wanted to apologize for, to explain. But he just couldn't bring himself to do it. He couldn't stand to see the certain recrimination in Amy's eyes, couldn't bear to see the dawning realization that her father's taunts of him being an unreliable no-account were absolutely dead on.

"We won't have to worry about it anyway," he said finally through tightly clenched jaws. "I mean, *she* is the one lying. She's not supposed to be here at all. Chances are if she sees us, she'll hide." His words sounded lame, even to his own ears, like he was trying to justify a lie. And Amy's silence made him all the more uncomfortable.

Obviously she didn't like being considered his date. Not that he blamed her. Every scornful thought she must hold toward him was well deserved. He knew he owed her an explanation; she deserved one. But he didn't want to explain, preferring instead to hold out hope that once this "date" was over and things with Shayna were squared away, they might find a way to become friends again. But the chance for that, after he told her the truth, was nil. He stood a better chance of walking barefoot on a bed of nails and coming out pain free.

Thankful to see the neon sign announcing the drive-in theater, he turned onto the well-lit gravel road that led to the box office. A cloud of dust rose and covered the truck in a haze.

"I just washed it," he grumbled.

"What?"

"Nothing." He didn't want Amy to think he was one of those guys who couldn't stand to see a speck of dust on the paint job.

Part of an old cow pasture, the drive-in doubled as the movie theater and a go-cart race track. When they drove up, the field was illuminated with floodlights. Several go-carts buzzed around in circles, their engines sounding like super-powered lawn mowers.

"It looks like there isn't a movie tonight after all." Amy sounded almost hopeful.

Quentin glanced at her. Did she want to go home already? The thought struck him with a pang of disappointment.

"Maybe we should have called first."

"No," Quentin said quickly. "They run the movies every night, just like when we used to come here together. I just wanted to get here extra early to scope out the parking lot."

"Ooooh. I see." The corners of her mouth quirked to match the teasing in her tone.

"Yes. Before you even say it, you're absolutely right. I do intend to park right behind her. If things get out of hand, Shayna will most definitely see me and know we're not here on a date."

There. He'd said it. Not a date. That should make her happy.

He turned from her to roll his window down and waited for the clerk to notice him. The brightness of the neon lights made him squint.

"Hey," said the teenage boy. He nodded at Quentin, the lights glinting off his black sunglasses. Quentin wondered why they had the lights so bright the employees had to shade their eyes.

"The movie won't start for an hour," the boy said.

"Do you mind if we pay now anyway and just park over there? We can find our spot for the movie later."

The kid shrugged and handed Quentin his change. "Suit yourself."

"Movies are still cheap here," Amy said as Quentin eased the truck away from the box office. "I read somewhere that there are very few drive-in theaters left in the country."

Nodding in response, Quentin was all too aware that it was merely small talk to cover for her—and his—discomfort over being at this place that suddenly had some pretty steamy memories assaulting his senses. They'd never actually made love, but the heated kisses, passionate embraces, and all the feelings and thoughts that lay in their hearts, certainly heightened the desire to do so. And it had always been difficult to stop. That was why he was so concerned about Shayna. He knew how quickly things could get out of hand and accelerate to something much more than just a few kisses. He trusted himself to hold back. But he certainly didn't trust the Baxter kid.

He backed the truck along the far side of the concession stand, certain he'd be able to see each and every car that came into the lot, and then switched off the ignition. The truck was bathed in a sudden, familiar, intimate darkness, making him even more uncomfortable.

"Those must be new." Amy pointed at the go-carts. Her voice was breathy and her hand fluttered. Quentin wondered if she was equally as uncomfortable.

"They've been here a few years. When the theater changed ownership, the new people sold off the cows and replaced them with these rinky-dink things."

"Have you ever tried them out?" There was mild interest in her tone.

Could she be hinting that she wanted to risk life and limb in one of those little contraptions? Or worse, maybe trying to find out how often he came here with a date. He didn't want to admit the answer, which was never.

"No," he said. "I don't see many men my age racing around this crazy little track."

"Hmm..." was all she said, and combined with her look of pure delight, that 'hmm' suggested the go-carts had alerted her sense of adventure.

"I'll go get us some popcorn." He hoped to divert her.

Amy raised one eyebrow. "Trying to change the subject?"

"No, I—"

"Chicken?"

Oh, no. He could see what was coming and

squeezed his eyes shut as if that would be enough to stop what he knew was about to happen.

"Eat my dust." With her challenge, Amy unfastened her seatbelt.

Quentin groaned. He didn't want to do this!

"Loser buys the popcorn." And with that, she was out of the truck and racing toward the go-cart booth.

Quentin followed her, loving her spirited, adventurous side. But at the same time, he dreaded folding his body into one of those contraptions. Go-carts weren't his style. A boat maybe, a hydroplane, even a man-sized race car. But not a go-cart. And yet, she'd issued him a challenge. He loved a challenge, and found it especially nice coming from Amy. Perhaps this wouldn't be so bad after all.

"Fifteen bucks," muttered the clerk, another teenage boy, around a cigarette. Quentin winced as the smoke hit him full in the face and wondered about the safety parameters concerning smoking around the little gas engines.

"Did you say fifteen bucks?"

"That's right. Fifteen bucks for ten minutes around the track."

"Ten minutes? That's it?"

"Believe me, mister." Quentin noticed an emphasis on mister, as if it were synonymous with old. "Ten minutes is all you'll want in one of these things."

He did believe it and wondered if there was a diplomatic way out of doing this. But Amy was already climbing into her little blue vehicle, so he sighed and handed over his fifteen bucks. No wonder the owners got rid of the cows. Go-cart racing must be much more lucrative than milking cows.

"Come on, Quentin. What's taking you so long?"

Amy was strapped in and fastening a motorcycle helmet over her short cap of hair. She was impassioned, vivacious, laughing, enticing. He swallowed hard and tore his eyes away. She might be enjoying herself right now, but he doubted she'd be able to get her cart headed in the right direction before their ten minutes were up.

ॐॐ

Amy felt more alive than she had in years. She felt young, carefree, happy. All the things she couldn't remember ever feeling in her adult life. It was great. She steered the little cart around the curves in the track then gave it more gas. It lurched as it picked up speed. Between the road noise and the vibration of the wheels on the bumpy track—not to mention the exhaust fumes, Amy felt like she was an Indy driver. Looking over her shoulder to smile at Quentin, she noticed he wasn't behind her.

No matter. He'd undoubtedly catch up. Men thought they were so much better at this sort of thing than women. Of course, Quentin hadn't been entirely thrilled with this idea of hers. Maybe he hated go-carts. Maybe he didn't know how to drive one. Maybe he wouldn't catch up with her. She laughed out loud, not sure why the thought made her feel so good.

There was something to be said for throwing caution to the wind, letting go and giving in to impulse. Amy was glad she had, and for the first time, she was actually glad she'd come back to town. That sense of trepidation was gone. She felt...content. This was right; this was where she was supposed to be, here, with Quentin, enjoying herself as if nothing bad had ever happened to separate them. Maybe they could eventually pick up where they left off. Joy and hope blossomed within her, and she sent a small thank-you heavenward.

"This is great," she shouted as she passed Quentin on the track. Not sure if he heard her over the buzzing whine of the engine, Amy looked over her shoulder. That was when she realized he was still sitting at the starting point. He'd never moved!

"Watch out!"

Startled, Amy jerked her head around to see that while looking over her shoulder she'd drifted into the path of an oncoming cart. She jerked the wheel hard to the right but was too late to avoid the collision. The impact was jarring, in spite of the low speed. As if in slow motion the two vehicles screamed and whined as they slid, in tandem, sideways across the track.

By the time they skidded to a halt, Amy sat there dazed, breathless, and feeling incredibly stupid.

Instinctively, she slipped her hand under the shoulder harness and rubbed it along her collarbone. It was sore, but not horribly so. She hated to think what might have happened if she hadn't been strapped in. True, the carts didn't achieve a high rate of speed, but there were dents where the two vehicles had met, and she knew they both could have been seriously hurt. Her gaze flew to the other driver, a teenage boy who looked horrified.

"Are you hurt?" She studied the boy, distressed that she hadn't even given him a thought until that moment.

"I'm fine," he gasped. "But lady, what were you thinking?"

She looked away from his prying eyes, her mind

grasping for an answer. Thinking? She'd been thinking about Quentin.

"I— I should have paid closer attention, I know." She started to apologize but he spoke again.

"Say, I know you. You're that new teacher at the high school, aren't you?" He sounded delighted, like he'd made some wonderful discovery.

Great. Just great. This was the last thing she needed. Had the kid seen Quentin? Would he make the connection and spread it around that a teacher was dating a parent? Swallowing hard, Amy nodded. "But please, I'd appreciate it if word of this didn't get around the school."

"Oh, I understand," the boy said eagerly. "Reckless driving isn't exactly something you want the kids to know about you. If you know what I mean."

Wincing, she nodded weakly. The sound of running footsteps, and her name being shouted repeatedly, saved her from coming up with an answer. Quentin. She looked up to see him racing toward her, frantic. Feeling teary-eyed all of a sudden, she fought down an urge to collapse in his arms. It was an instinctual urge, she knew, because he was male with big strong shoulders meant for comforting a woman. That's all it was. Instinct.

"Amy, are you OK?" He unfastened her harness with trembling fingers, his brow creased in concern. "Can you stand?"

"Yes, of course." She did, with his help, and then he halfway guided, halfway lifted her out. He pulled her close and, instinct or no, she leaned willingly against his shoulders savoring his warm strength as it surrounded her. Inhaling the pleasing, comforting, familiar scent of his aftershave, she was reminded of a dozen other times when he'd held her like this.

"Amy, I'm so relieved. When I saw the crash, I—"
He broke off and merely stared into her eyes like he
was trying to soak her up. She swallowed hard. The
look in his eyes was more than concern, and if she ever
doubted he'd once cared for her, she didn't any longer.

"Ma'am, are you OK?" Amy looked over
Quentin's shoulder to see the youth who'd outfitted
her with the go-cart. Before she could assure the boy
that she was OK, an older gentleman raced up behind
him.

Out of breath from running, the man's words
came out in a wheeze. "What happened here? Is
anybody hurt?" He pulled a hanky out of his pocket
and mopped the glistening sweat from his forehead,
while studying Amy with a worried expression.

"I'm afraid I was looking over my shoulder
instead of paying attention." Amy stepped out of
Quentin's arms to face the man, who was most likely
the owner. She shivered, suddenly chilly, and
swallowed hard. "I guess I drifted in front of the other
cart."

"Well, ma'am." The gentleman looked slightly
nervous as he patted his brow with his handkerchief
again. "Pardon me for saying this, but a little thing like
you, maybe you should watch from the sidelines next
time. The track can be dangerous if you don't know
what you're doing."

If he hadn't been so sincere, so concerned, Amy
might have been offended at what he was suggesting.
She knew he meant no harm though, so she merely
nodded.

Beside her, Quentin cleared his throat. "I'll be glad
to pay for any damage."

"No, Quentin," she said in a rush. "It was my fault and I'll take care of it."

"Well, look here," said the owner. "A few dents are no big deal. My youngest son likes fiddling with these things, and he'll be happy to have something to mess around with. No one's hurt, and that's the important thing."

"Can I finish my ride, mister?" The boy Amy collided with was back in his vehicle, looking anxious to be on his way.

"Sure thing. In fact, why don't you take an extra ten minutes on the track? Randy?" He turned to the teenager who'd been in charge of assigning carts. "You see that this fellow gets some extra time, OK?"

Randy nodded and shuffled off in the direction of the starting line, and the teenager took off in his cart with a backward wave at Amy. Oh, she hoped he kept his mouth shut at school on Monday morning.

"Now then, why don't you two come on up to my office and I'll treat you to a nice hot cup of coffee."

"That would be nice, thanks." Amy didn't drink coffee, but she didn't want to hurt the man's feelings so she started to follow him off the track.

Before she could leave, Quentin reached out and grasped her by the shoulders. She turned and looked at him, confused.

"She'll be right along sir," he called to the man. "She just needs a minute to collect herself."

"I don't—"

"Shh. I do." And with that, Quentin drew her into his arms. His lips gently brushed hers, tenderly, petal soft at first.

Only a heartbeat passed before Amy relaxed in his arms and gave in to the urge to wrap her arms around his back. In doing so, she pulled him closer, reveling in the weak-kneed feelings that encompassed her as he deepened the kiss. And when he did, she was swept back to high school just as if the intervening seventeen years had never happened. Just as if the world was, as it had been then, full of hope and golden promise.

Just Quentin and her, together again.

6

The kiss, that wonderful, soul-stirring kiss, changed everything. Quentin may have felt nothing but protectiveness toward her, but Amy knew in that one instant that she'd never stopped loving him.

Dare she even hope he felt something for her? Yes. She dared. She hoped. And her heart soared much like it did when she received her very first kiss from him back in the tenth grade.

He held her hand as they made their way to the little office at the back of the drive-in's concession stand, and stood protectively beside her while she sipped the bitter coffee Mr. Owens insisted she needed to calm her 'feminine' nerves. In spite of the fact that she knew he was chomping at the bit to get back to the truck so they could watch for Shayna, Quentin made polite small talk with the man. Maybe he sensed that Mr. Owens needed his own nerves calmed down.

Either way, she admired his good manners. He displayed those manners again, when they arrived back at the truck, insisting she needed something to eat, despite her protests to the contrary. Then, after seeing she was seated comfortably in the truck, he ran back to the concession stand.

Now, sitting alone in the plush interior of Quentin's truck while she awaited his return, one thing was certain. Crystal clear. She had to let Jared know there was no future for them. Even if she left Goose

Bay today, tonight, and never looked back, Quentin Macmillan would always hold the key to her heart. To give less to another man would be wrong, and she could never do something so cruel to a man as good and decent as Jared.

The kiss, followed by the tender way he'd held her hand as they walked to Mr. Owens's office, had flooded her soul with memories of tenderness and passion. She wondered if Quentin felt the same way.

As Quentin neared the truck, she stretched across the seat and opened his door. He caught it with his hip and held it that way while Amy took the tray with the sodas and hot dogs. Quentin plopped two tubs of popcorn next to her and climbed in. Amy sniffed deeply, inhaling the heavenly smells of popcorn and hot dogs, and felt like a kid again. Movie food. Not her normal everyday fare, but perhaps that made it all the more heavenly.

Once he was settled and they were munching contentedly, Amy asked, "What kind of car are we looking for?"

"I'm not too sure," Quentin said. "We'll just have to watch and see if we can spot them or watch for them to go and get snacks. Surely they'll be doing that."

"Of course. Snacks and teenagers just sort of go together."

With the illumination of the floodlights still lighting the area, it was easy to watch each car as it pulled in, searching for Shayna and her friends. At least that's what she thought until one by one, low riding cars and small pickup trucks with tinted windows and loud thumping music rolled and bounced past them in search of a parking spot.

"I sure hope she isn't in one of those," Quentin

grumbled.

Amy hoped not either. If Shayna happened to be in a car with dark windows, there'd be no way to spot her. With the tight set of his jaw, she could practically hear Quentin's teeth grind together. She pictured him whipping car doors open in search of his daughter.

Quentin stirred agitatedly in his seat. Amy put her hand on his arm, as much to calm herself as him. He shrugged away from her touch. Along with the sting of rejection, a thousand doubts assailed her. He'd been right when he said this was her fault. If she'd separated Shayna from Bradley when Quentin first asked her to, none of this would be happening.

Dear Lord, she prayed silently, *please keep Shayna safe. And please, Lord, I don't want to feel this way any longer. Help me realize I don't belong here. I don't want to be rejected like I was when I was a teenager. Help me forget the kiss we shared, help me put the past, and Quentin, behind me and walk away from here.*

"That's them," Quentin said when he spotted a mini-van full of girls. Shayna sat directly behind the driver, laughing animatedly. Amy didn't recognize anyone else in the van, though she was sure Ashley was in there somewhere.

Quentin started the truck and flipped on the parking lights.

"As soon as they park, I'll grab the spot behind them."

They watched until the van finally eased into a spot several rows from the concession stand. Quentin took a sip of his soda before he shot Amy a smile.

"Well," he said looking pleased. "No one is parking nearby so maybe they weren't planning anything after all."

"I hope you're—" Amy broke off as a battleship-sized car that appeared to be a relic from the late sixties or early seventies pulled up next to the girls. She watched in horror as four boys jumped from the car and piled into the van. One of them was Bradley Baxter.

"That's it." Quentin jerked his hand from hers and thrust his drink at Amy. "Hold this."

Before she had a chance to react, Quentin had the truck in gear and was lurching forward. Popcorn and soda went everywhere. "Quentin!" She squealed and made a frantic grab for the sodas, but ice and sticky pop rushed over her jeans like a tidal wave. Quentin didn't seem to notice as he tore across the bumpy field and bore down on the space directly behind the kids. Sighing in disgust, Amy grabbed the napkins and began mopping up as best she could.

This father was about to ruin his relationship with his daughter, and she had wet pants. There must be some humor in this somewhere. If only it weren't so tragic.

"Now what are you going to do, Quentin?" Amy tried to keep her tone soft as he hit yet another bump. "Lock her in her room for the rest of her life?"

"Yes, as a matter of fact I will."

"No," she said gently. "Remember what we talked about? It will only backfire, and you'll make her more determined to see Bradley. That's not what you want. Take a deep breath, calm down. If she sees you, remember to act natural. You're on a date, and you don't notice anything amiss. Got that?"

He nodded. He might not be happy, but Amy was sure this was the best way. Things would be OK. Or so she thought until a teenager in a sports car cut right in front of him and pulled into the space he wanted. He blared on the horn, and the kid and his companions stuck their arms out the windows and made rude gestures.

"Same to you, punk."

"Quentin!"

"Well," he said in a defensive tone. "How am I supposed to keep an eye on her now?"

"Just pull in here, Quentin, it'll be fine. Just fine. You'll be able to see good enough." Amy rolled her eyes. Perhaps it really was a good thing she was along. Keeping Quentin in line was a job all its own. Imagine what would have happened if she wasn't here? He'd probably end up in jail for harassing Bradley.

Quentin pulled in to the space she'd indicated, all the while muttering under his breath. Amy half expected him to jump out and storm the girls' van. Instead he helped scoop up ice cubes and mop up soda, all the while grumbling something she couldn't hear.

"Would you like me to run and get you another drink?"

She shuddered. "No. Not if you're going to spill it all over me again."

"I'm sorry, Amy. Really I am. I don't know what came over me. As soon as I saw the boys get into the van I lost sight of everything except pounding some heads together. Forgive me?"

She looked at him, saw the earnestness in his eyes, and felt some invisible hand pluck the strings of her heart. Smiling with all the tenderness that filled her, she nodded.

"Here, how about if you sit on my jacket. That wet seat can't be too comfortable."

Amy protested as he reached behind his seat and produced a brown bomber jacket. "Oh Quentin, I couldn't. It's leather. It would be ruined."

"I don't know about that. I'm sure it could be cleaned. Besides, it's my fault anyway. If I hadn't had that momentary lapse of reason, you wouldn't be sitting here shivering." When he held the jacket out to her, he stole another piece of her heart. "Take it."

"Thank you."

Once she was settled back into her seat, the warmth from his jacket beginning to ease some of the chill from her soda-soaked pants, she sighed and tried to concentrate on the silly pizza advertisements that played on the screen. It wasn't easy. Her thoughts kept drifting to Quentin, to the kiss they'd shared. It was too good to be true. Most likely, it meant nothing to him.

Stealing a side-glance at him, she saw he had his eyes glued to the girls' van. It was obvious by the set of his jaw they would remain that way. This was a totally different side of him, one she'd never expected to see. It wasn't bad, she decided. To a casual observer Quentin might appear to be overreacting, but she knew what was in his heart, and it touched her deeply. He was a loving father doing whatever he could to make sure his daughter was safe.

She would have done the same thing in his position. How, she wondered, would it have been if they were here at the drive-in keeping an eye on their daughter? It was a pointless way to think, because the past could not be changed. No matter how much she wanted it to be so, Shayna was not her daughter. She was Karen's. Quentin's and Karen's. The past was over and nothing could change it. In spite of that knowledge, she still yearned for answers. Part of her did, anyway. The other part of her wasn't so sure she *did* want to know why Quentin had never showed that night.

That he'd suddenly decided Karen was the one for him wasn't what she wanted to hear. But she did want to know if Karen made him happy, if they'd had a good family life, that sort of thing. She sat up straight and took a deep breath, mustering the nerve to act casual and drop it into the conversation.

He looked at her just then and smiled. She lost all nerve. She couldn't ask, didn't want to know, and certainly didn't want to risk him comparing her, the loser, to Karen, the winner.

Winner, loser. The words reverberated through her mind in an evil, irritating manner.

When the door to the van in front of them flew open, and Shayna jumped out followed by Bradley, Quentin was out of the truck before Amy could react. Stunned, she watched as he stormed toward the kids swaggering like a macho thug spoiling for a fight.

It's OK. It'll be fine. She'd just hop out of the truck and stand beside him, a gentle reminder that she hoped would help divert an ugly confrontation. Rounding the truck to catch up with Quentin, she tried to forget about the wet soda stain on her jeans. It was dark, the kids wouldn't notice anyway.

"Daddy," Shayna squealed. She sounded delighted to see her father, not affronted by the fact that he was spying on her. She didn't even seem to jump to that conclusion. "What are you doing here?"

"I'm on a date. What are you doing here? And why are you with him?" He jerked his thumb at Bradley. "You're supposed to be at Ashley's."

"Hey, Mr. Macmillan." Bradley stuck his hand out

to Quentin, appearing a lot more confident than he sounded. "Bradley Baxter. I worked for you last summer, remember?" His voice cracked on the last word, and he swallowed hard, visibly nervous now.

"Oh, Baxter, yes." Quentin's laugh sounded forced, and he ignored the outstretched hand. "Now I remember. How's it going?" Before Bradley could respond, Quentin ushered Shayna away from Bradley.

The boy stared after them and then looked down at his hand. Amy thought she detected a flush creep up his neck, but it may have been a reflection from the colors on the movie screen. He shrugged, stuck his hand in his pocket and finally looked at Amy.

"Hello Bradley," she said.

"Miss Welsh." He nodded then looked miserably over to where Quentin was questioning Shayna. He may have taken her off to the side, but they could still hear every word he said.

"Shayna, I thought you were spending the night at Ashley's. Do you girls come here often?"

"No. Ashley's sister offered to bring us to the drive-in. Her mom said it was OK. Honest. Then we saw some boys in our class, and they wanted to sit with us. Honest, that's all. We're just watching the movie together. I mean," she lowered her voice, "I'm not interested in dating or anything like that, you know."

Bradley stared at the ground and kicked his foot back and forth a few times, obviously distressed by Shayna's declaration. "She has to say that," he muttered. "Her dad hates me. I don't think he'll ever forgive me."

"I don't think he hates you," Amy said in a rush. He seemed genuinely upset and she wanted to reassure him. Her heart went out to the poor guy. It can't be easy—listening to the girl you're interested in deny she's interested in you. "Forgiveness is harder for some than others. Especially fathers."

"The thing is, I really like her. When she first asked me to—" He broke off as though he was about to reveal some deep dark secret. What? That Shayna had asked him out? Girls did that all the time. "I mean—at first she was just an ordinary girl. But now—there's something special about her. You know what I mean?"

Amy nodded, and Bradley looked at his toes, as if embarrassed to have revealed so much.

But what exactly had he revealed? That he liked Shayna. That perhaps he hadn't been very interested in her at first, but now he was. And she may have been the one to ask him out.

He didn't seem to be the kind of kid who would intentionally break a girl's heart. But Amy knew from experience how well some guys could hide that part of their nature.

She looked back over at Quentin, who was fidgeting back and forth. Amy could tell he really wanted to pop Bradley in the jaw and drag his daughter kicking and screaming back home. When he caught her eye, something in his expression must have captured Shayna's attention because she turned and finally noticed Amy.

"Hey, Miss Welsh! Dad, why didn't you tell me you're dating her? Cool!" She gave her dad a playful punch in the arm then flashed a huge smile at Amy. "We have to go order the pizzas. Way to go, Dad!" Before Quentin could respond, Shayna and Bradley were running up the field toward the concession stand. Amy was sure Bradley was glad to have escaped unscathed.

"That went pretty well." Quentin looked quite pleased with himself as they climbed back in the truck. "Don't you think?"

"You mean because you didn't punch his lights out?"

"I thought I controlled myself very well." The grin he flashed her was boyish, reminiscent of the boy she once knew. Her heart leaped.

"You did," she agreed.

"So why do I feel so empty?" The grin faded, and his tone changed drastically, more in keeping with a father who'd just discovered he wasn't the most important man in his daughter's life.

His heart was breaking, she realized with a jolt. So was hers. Because she didn't want him to hurt. She wanted to spare him any pain he might encounter in his life. Acting on pure instinct as she had earlier when she'd willingly gone into his arms, she reached out and grabbed his hand. He laced his fingers with hers and clasped her palm against his. Oh what was she doing? This was dangerous ground. *Be careful,* she warned herself. *You could get your heart broken again.*

Still, in spite of every warning she could think to give herself, she leaned into his side as he walked with her to the passenger side of the truck.

That warning was quickly forgotten, though, when Quentin leaned against the passenger door of his truck, pulling her with him. She fell gently against his rock-solid chest, her hand still clasped in his.

With his free hand, he cradled the back of her head, tilting her face to meet his.

This was nice; this was right. Amy gazed up at him and felt a thrill course through her as she glimpsed the raw emotion lighting his eyes. Her breath quickened as their lips met, and she closed her eyes with a sigh.

If the way he kissed was any indication, Quentin felt the same thing she did. She sighed in pleasure, nestling her hand further into his.

Loud giggles broke through Amy's consciousness. The mini-van. Shayna's friends—some of them Amy's students. She pushed away from Quentin in alarm.

"Amy, what—?"

"Shh. Just get in the truck. Hurry. They're laughing at us."

After a measured glance at the van in front of them, Quentin nodded then helped her into the truck. She didn't really need help, but the contact was nice, and perhaps it was his way of assuring them both that this wasn't their last kiss.

"So what do we do now?" she asked nervously when they were settled back in the truck.

"Now, I quit worrying about my little girl and start concentrating on my date."

"But you don't have a date."

"I just told my daughter I did. You wouldn't want to make me out to be a liar now, would you?"

"But Quentin, the whole idea was for us to keep our eyes on Shayna in case anything got out of control."

He took her hand, caressing her senses with a warm tingly feeling. "I guess I'd just rather stay in the dark. If my daughter was going to run off behind the refreshment stand with that Baxter character, I've already put a stop to it, and I'd rather not know what their real plans might have been."

"I'm proud of you, Quentin. One would never

know from your conversation that you can't stand the kid."

"Is that right?" He beamed. "Well, maybe, just maybe, I'm not as bad as you thought."

He didn't let go of her hand when he slumped down to get more comfortable and watch the movie. But when Shayna knocked on the window on her way back to the van with her pizza, he dropped it and didn't pick it up again. Amy felt a little disappointed but tried not to show it. They weren't here to make eyes at each other. They were here for Shayna who didn't need them anymore.

There was nothing left for Amy to do but try and concentrate on the movie.

The kids didn't stay for the second movie. Amy could almost feel Quentin's relief when the boys climbed out of the van and got into their own car. When the girls took off, they honked and waved at Quentin and Amy and were noisily followed by the boys. A few other cars got into the exit line, and Quentin waited until the girls were halfway down the road before he turned the engine on. "You didn't want to stay and see this movie, did you?"

Truthfully, she didn't even know what the second movie was. And no, she didn't want to watch it, but neither did she want her time with Quentin to come to an end. So, yes, she was disappointed.

"I'm sorry, I didn't hear you."

"No," Amy mumbled. She was upset with herself for feeling so down all of a sudden.

"Good. Because as soon as I make sure Shayna arrives safe and sound at Ashley's house, we're going for a drive."

A drive? "Where?"

"You'll see," was all he'd say. He looked over at her and grinned, and apprehension assailed her. What was Quentin planning?

They parked down the street from Ashley's house and watched as the girls raced through the door. Satisfied his daughter wouldn't be up to any further mischief that night, Quentin finally pulled away from the curb. As he headed south out of town, Amy's apprehension grew.

"Quentin, where are we going?"

"Be patient. I said you'll see." His answering grin told her everything she needed to know.

"No." She said it plainly, but firmly. "Take me home."

"What?" Quentin looked at her, askance.

"I said take me home." Her insides were shaking, but she managed to keep her tone even. "I'm not ready for a drive down memory lane."

His sheepish grin told her she was right in her assumptions. Quentin was planning to take her on a nighttime tour of all their old haunts. She couldn't. She still felt all the same feelings toward him. For her nothing had changed. For him everything had. There was no going back, and to look back would be like salting a gaping wound.

"I can't do it, Quentin. Please take me home now." She prayed her voice sounded natural, even though she felt anything but.

Suddenly, Amy wished she'd never come back to town.

7

"Come on." Quentin shook a couple of lettuce leaves at Rufus and tried to coax the duck over.

Rufus eyed the lettuce, his head titled to one side. Finally he took a slow cautious step forward, then another, waddling from one side to the next until he stood before Quentin—and more importantly, before the lettuce. Dropping the green leaves to the ground, Quentin laughed softly. This was their daily pattern, and every morning—even after two years—Rufus still approached him with caution.

While the duck nibbled eagerly, Quentin leaned against the house and watched with less than his usual enthusiasm and pleasure. He and Shayna had yet to discuss the boys and the drive-in. Yesterday, when she'd come home from the slumber party, she was strangely quiet and had shut herself up in her room. He'd hoped to discuss it this morning, but now Shayna was so late there wouldn't be time to talk about it before church.

Impatiently, he glanced at his watch. What had she been thinking about, sneaking off to the movie like that? True, she'd said Ashley's mom had given them permission, but he knew without a doubt Ashley's mom didn't know a group of boys figured into the mix. Maybe he should have a talk with Mrs. Morgan after church.

Foster, Mrs. Parson's old tomcat, leaped down

from the top of the fence to slink across the yard. Knowing Rufus could hold his own, Quentin sat on the picnic bench to see what would happen. While he waited, his thoughts drifted to Amy.

Why had she cut their evening short Friday night? Oh, he knew why—he just didn't want to admit it. She'd said she didn't want to reminisce, but he knew it was because helping him with Shayna was the only reason she'd agreed to be in his presence. Clearly, she was still angry after all these years. And she deserved to be. He owed her an explanation. As much as he didn't want to face up to the past, he intended to see she got it. Just as soon as he worked up the nerve.

He found himself wanting to prolong the talk for more reasons than just lack of courage. Friday night had warmed something in him. Rekindled a forgotten memory. A memory of more than just the passion of a few heated kisses. It was a memory of friendship, laughter, understanding. The sharing of dreams, hopes, the innocence with which they beheld their future. If only they'd known how things would turn out between them...would they have been so happy then?

Not that Quentin had any regrets with regard to his life with Karen. He'd loved her wholly—done his best to make her happy and he knew she'd done the same. And they had a beautiful daughter as a result. The light of his life. Regrets? No. His only regret came with the way his relationship with Amy had ended. That and the things that lay unspoken between them.

At least he'd been able to spend a few hours in her presence. Talking, getting to know each other again. What more could he want?

Yes, Amy would get her explanation. Then she'd

never speak to him again.

Foster chose that moment to pounce, disrupting both his thoughts and Rufus's meal. Rufus quacked once, loudly, as Foster nearly ended up with a mouthful of feathers. Then he jumped forward and snagged a piece of orange fur in his beak. Foster yowled and the chase was on. If he'd told anyone that a cat was running from a duck, they wouldn't believe him.

The interruption was for the best, he knew. There were more important things to think about. Like his daughter. What kind of parent was he, anyway— thinking about lost romance when his daughter's shenanigans should be taking precedence? Karen would have been very disappointed in him. But no more disappointed than he was in himself.

⇝⇜

"Hey Quentin, I heard you had a date Friday night." Russ cornered him as soon as he and Shayna stepped out of the church pew.

Russ. Good. They needed to talk. Quentin was just about to suggest they get together later in the afternoon when he noticed Mrs. Parsons. A few feet ahead of them, she turned and stared. Her eyes lit with interest at Russ's comment. Before Quentin could react to anything, Shayna was off like lighting.

"Shayna! We're leaving soon!"

She never turned around, merely melted into a crowd of teenagers gathered at the back of the sanctuary.

He glanced at Mrs. P., and then turned his back on her—hoping she'd get the hint and continue on her way. The last thing he needed was his nosy neighbor bugging him about his love life—or lack thereof.

"Thanks a lot, Russ," he grumbled. "Now it'll be all over church."

Elbowing him in the ribs, Russ spoke a little too loud. "So, how was it?"

"Keep your voice down." Quentin looked over his shoulder, concerned about the topic of conversation. Sure enough Mrs. P. was still standing there, eyebrows lifted, her eyes glittering. "It wasn't a date."

How had Russ heard about it anyway?

"Heard it was a new teacher..."

Quentin pressed his lips together and inhaled sharply, waiting for Russ to make the connection.

"...someone by the name of Amy Welsh. Hey!"

Quentin exhaled in a huff, and then winced as a glimmer of recognition settled in Russ's eyes. His friend had made the connection.

"Is she the same Amy Welsh you were so tight with in school?"

"It wasn't a date," Quentin repeated through clenched teeth.

"Your old girlfriend, a night at the drive-in. Yeah, right. If it wasn't a date, then what was it?"

"We were only—" He broke off. What could he say? Admit to spying on his daughter? Then word would get out that Quentin couldn't control his daughter, that she was trouble. He knew Russ would never say it like that, but word traveled quick in Goose Bay and it always ended up twisted to the worst degree. He'd end up with more than just a ribbing and a practical joke from the guys at work.

"Think what you want," he groused to his friend. "Just keep your mouth shut."

"Hey." Russ held up his hands. "No problem. But I guess this means there's no hope for you and my sister."

There never was, but Quentin didn't say it.

"When are you going to see her again?"

I'm not, Quentin thought. At least not for a date. He did need to talk to her again—just once more. He owed it to her. Ashamed as he was of the reason he never showed up, she deserved the truth. Not that he planned to tell Russ about it.

"I've got to go find my daughter." Before he left, Quentin poked Russ in the chest. "*Don't* open your mouth about this." He jabbed his finger at Russ one more time for emphasis. "To anyone."

"How did Russ Miller know I was at the drive-in with Amy?"

They were in the truck, still in the church parking lot. Shayna looked away from Quentin, but not quickly enough to hide the guilt that registered on her face.

"Shayna." He titled his head, squared his jaw and raised an eyebrow.

She was quiet for a moment, and then turned to him with a smile that was clearly meant to push all his buttons. "Can we get pizza for lunch?"

"Don't change the subject. I want to know how Russ knew."

"Tell me if we can get the pizza, then I'll tell you."

"Fine," he relented. She'd only manage to wear him down if he didn't give in. And today he was too tired for her theatrics. "Now how did Russ find out?"

Shayna stirred uncomfortably and turned back to her window.

"I don't know." Her voice was pitched unusually high.

"Shayna, what have I taught you about lying? More importantly, what have you learned in church about lying?"

"Daddy!" She sounded outraged.

"Well?" Sometimes kids could be so exasperating.

"Rusty Miller was one of the boys at the drive-in," she finally said.

"So you decided to *tell* Rusty I was there on a date?" Quentin considered the implications here. First that Rusty knew he'd been on a date with Amy and most likely told his dad. Second that Russ knew he used to date Amy and half the town, not to mention the church, would soon know he'd been on a date. And more importantly, they'd know his daughter had been to the drive-in with boys. He saw red.

"No pizza." He shoved the truck into gear and lurched out of the parking space.

"But, Dad—"

"No buts about it. I'm so angry with you right now, I just need to think. And," he added pointedly as he eased out of the parking lot and onto the narrow road that led back to town, "you'd better keep your mouth quiet while I do."

"Think about what?" She sounded oh-so-innocent, but Quentin knew she was goading him.

"Think about whether or not I should lock you in your room for the rest of your natural life, that's what!" As soon as he spoke, Quentin was sorry. He swallowed hard and tried to find the words to apologize to his daughter.

Instead, he slowly guided the truck back into town and toward Alfredo's Pizza.

They were almost there when Shayna broke the silence. "Can I talk now?"

Quentin looked over at his daughter and smiled. "What am I going to do with you?"

"I don't know, Dad. Just love me, I guess." She laughed a deep, infectious laugh he never grew tired of hearing. "But if you're finished being mad, I need to remind you of something."

"What's that?"

"*You* were the one who told me you were on a date. And you never said not to tell anyone."

She had him there. She was so good at twisting him around her finger. Good thing he only had one daughter to contend with.

"You really like her, huh Dad?" She sounded much too enthusiastic, and Quentin didn't know what to make of it. Did his daughter *want* him to date? He'd always heard horror stories about teens that went out of their way to sabotage their parents' dates.

"Did anyone ever tell you that you ask too many questions?"

"Yeah, you." She reached over and gave him a playful punch on the arm.

"Well, it's my turn to ask a question, OK?"

"Sure, Dad."

"How did you know Miss Welsh and I used to date in high school?"

"She told you about that, huh?" Shayna's lips twitched in a half-smile that Quentin found a little odd.

"Yes, she did."

"Mrs. Morgan."

"That's what I thought. What else did she tell you?"

"Just that you really liked each other and that everyone thought you'd end up getting married."

Struck by a pang of guilt over the past, Quentin

was glad Shayna was quiet for a minute. It gave him time to gather his thoughts before she asked the inevitable next question.

"So, how come you didn't?"

He sighed, not wanting to think about the answer. "Sweetheart, some questions are better left unasked. This is one of them."

"So you're not going to answer me, huh?"

"Nope." He shook his head. "And I don't want you to ask me again." Was it his imagination, or did Shayna look much too pleased with herself?

૭∾৹

Amy closed her Bible and ran her hand over the textured cover. The leather was soft and cool to the touch. Comforting. Still, she felt sick at heart.

Ever since she'd moved back to Goose Bay, she'd avoided going to church. Not that she didn't want to go. It was just so hard to walk into a church that first time and feel comfortable. Not because she didn't know a lot of people here, but because she just hadn't worked up the courage—until today.

After Miki's mention of the potluck the other day, and knowing a friend would be there, Amy finally felt ready to go to church on Sunday morning. She needed the fellowship, the singing, needed to be with other Christians.

She was finally ready to start over.

So she headed to the tiny church on the outskirts of town and pulled into the parking lot in time to see Quentin getting out of his truck with Shayna. Why, out of all the churches in Goose Bay, had she chosen the one he attended? It had never even occurred to her.

She'd put the car in reverse and backed out of the parking lot and headed home.

Now she sat at her kitchen table feeling like a wimp. No, worse. A marshmallow. Unable to walk into a church because Quentin was there.

Now she'd have to wait another week for the opportunity to worship and praise the Lord in the company of fellow Christians. Another week of butterflies and anxiety over walking into a new church—and it wouldn't be the one where Quentin Macmillan worshipped.

She stood up and began to pace. Whenever she got angry at herself or anyone else for that matter, her tendency was to get moving. Certain a good brisk walk would help her feel better, she rummaged through the closet for her walking shoes and in a matter of minutes was out the door in the fresh air.

The sun was out. A pleasant and far cry from the usual spring afternoon in the Pacific Northwest. Amy walked down the country road with no particular destination in mind. Though she lived outside the city limits in what was termed 'the country', she was really only a couple of miles from the center of town. Half an hour later she found herself downtown and by the stream of traffic, she figured church had just ended. She felt the pang in her stomach again and increased her pace.

"Amy!"

She turned at the sound of her name, and her stomach lurched when she saw Shayna just emerging from her dad's truck. Amy wasn't used to such blatant disrespect from her students and if they'd been in the classroom, she would have corrected Shayna. But here, in town, on a Sunday afternoon, Amy didn't feel up to a confrontation. Especially not in front of Quentin.

When Shayna waved, Amy returned it reluctantly and hoped Quentin hadn't seen her. He seemed preoccupied with his CDs or the CD player. She turned to go, hoping Shayna would get the hint and let Amy continue with her walk.

"Amy, I mean, Miss Welsh! Come here!"

One could hardly ignore a shouting fourteen-year-old. They would just get louder and could outlast most adults. She felt a pang of sympathy for Quentin. It couldn't be easy, raising a teenager on your own. Dutifully, but not happily, Amy stepped toward the truck.

"Dad says it's rude to call you by your first name. But I figured since you two know each other, it might be OK."

Amy didn't know what to say, so she kept silent.

"We just got out of church, and now we're getting some pizza. Do you want some?"

Amy shook her head. "I don't think—"

"Come on, Miss Welsh. Join us."

She looked up at the sound of Quentin's voice. She shot him a glare, hoping Shayna couldn't interpret it. Why was he doing this to her when he clearly knew she didn't want to see him again? Well, she amended, she did want to see him, but her heart couldn't bear it.

"No," she said with regret. "I really can't." Feeling worse than she did when she started out on the walk, she turned and started away.

"Amy, please?" His voice was gentle, the tones washed over her, melting her heart.

She slowed her pace, hesitating.

"Pepperoni, lightly-sauced. Your favorite."

She stopped in her tracks.

If he hadn't remembered her favorite, she would have kept on walking. How, after all these years, had he managed to remember her favorite pizza and the way she liked it ordered? *The same way he'd remembered Dr. Pepper was her favorite drink.* Touched, she turned and her gaze collided with his heart-stopping smile. She looked up into his crystal blue eyes and was totally lost. Unable to help herself, she nodded slowly then followed them into the pizza parlor.

The years drifted away as they walked through the old-fashioned swinging doors. It seemed like yesterday that she was here with Quentin and a rowdy band of their friends, playing the pinball machines and records on the jukebox. Of course now the jukebox played CDs and the pinball machines had been replaced by video game systems. But it didn't matter. The atmosphere was the same; noisy shouts and laughter, the clanging of pizza pans in the kitchen, and the garlicky, yeasty smell of fresh baked pizza.

She smiled, feeling shy though secretly pleased as she stood beside Quentin while he ordered the pizza just the way she liked it. If he noticed the gagging noises his daughter made when the clerk read back the order, he ignored it. Again she felt that pang of sympathy for him.

Following Quentin and Shayna to the soda fountain where they had to fill their own drinks, she glanced around the restaurant.

Alfredo's. This had been their place. Hers and Quentin's. It had been here, at a candlelit table in a darkened corner, where Quentin had kissed her for the first time. They'd been eating pizza and garlic bread, laughing shyly. He'd risen from his seat across from her, and come around to sit beside her. She'd just taken another bite of her garlic bread when he'd leaned forward and kissed her. She'd been embarrassed, but not enough that she hadn't recognized the hint of promised passion behind the sweet and gentle touch of his lips on hers.

"Watch out!" Quentin shouted at the same time she felt sticky soda spilling over her hand. She'd been so carried away with memories, she'd overfilled her glass.

"Clumsy me." She laughed softly, trying to cover her embarrassment. Quentin was quick to grab some napkins and gently placed them over her hand, trying to wipe up the soda. She smiled her thanks, and picked up her drink.

"So, have you been to church?" Amy asked Shayna as they walked to the table. Of course, it was merely her way of making conversation, since she already knew they'd been, but she had to do something to concentrate on the present.

"Yeah, we go every Sunday. Dad teaches a Bible class in the mornings and sometimes leads the youth group on Sunday nights." She stopped talking only long enough to take a few slurps of her soda. "Tonight though, it's Mr. Miller's turn. He works for my dad."

"So your dad *makes* him teach Bible class in order to keep his job?" Amy raised her eyebrows in a teasing manner.

"Oh no," Shayna said around her straw. "They're best friends."

Quentin gave Amy a quirky little smile and rolled his eyes. Embarrassed by his daughter? Or embarrassed for her to know he taught Bible class?

"What age do you teach?" she asked, trying to make him feel more at ease.

"Whatever age there's a need for. Right now it's Kindergarten through first grade. And it isn't easy."

"No. I don't suppose it is." Amy laughed. "Five and six year olds are an interesting bunch, to say the least."

"You sound like you have experience."

"I do." She smiled. "I taught first grade before I moved here."

"First grade in church? Or first grade in school?"

"School. I've never taught a Bible class."

"Don't you go to church, Miss Welsh?" Amy was touched by the sudden concern in Shayna's eyes.

"Yes." She smiled. "But I haven't attended anywhere since I moved here. I am a Christian, though, and I'm sure I'll find a church soon."

"Maybe you can go with us sometime." Before Amy could answer, the clerk called their number.

"I'll get it!" Shayna jumped up and scrambled toward the counter.

"How come you haven't gone to church since you moved here?" Quentin spoke softly, almost as if concerned. Like father, like daughter.

"I've just been getting settled, that's all." She thought back to this morning, how she'd chickened out. "Really," she assured him as well as herself. She looked away and took a sip of her Dr. Pepper.

The warmth of Quentin's hand startled her when he covered hers with his. She continued to stare out the window at passing cars. One look into his eyes while he touched her hand, and she'd be lost. Headed for another heartbreak.

"Amy," he said softly. "Would you like to go to church with us tonight?"

"That's a cool idea," Shayna declared. She plopped

the pizza on the table. Quentin dropped Amy's hand.

It would be perfect. She wouldn't be walking into a building full of strangers all alone. But a sudden dread in the pit of her stomach held her back. "Um, I don't think I can tonight."

"I'm sorry to hear that," Quentin said. "Sunday nights are usually informal. We do devotions and sing. It's very relaxing, and very uplifting. I think you'd enjoy it."

"I'm sure I would."

"Then why don't you come?"

"I'll think about it."

"This is like eating a grilled cheese sandwich," Shayna grumbled around a mouthful of pizza.

"Kids." Quentin shook his head as he watched his daughter head toward the counter to ask for some more sauce. "Oh, by the way, the mystery is solved."

"What mystery?"

"The one where Shayna found out about our past."

"Who told her?"

"Just as I thought, it was Ashley's mom."

"Oh, yes. The one you said was good friends with Karen." Suddenly uncomfortable, Amy shifted in her seat.

"That's right. Hey, I have to take Shayna by there to pick up one of her schoolbooks. *And* to speak with Ashley's mom about those boys and the drive-in. I know she'd love to see you again. You want to ride along?"

"No, thank you." Meet a woman who had been one of Karen's close friends? Amy didn't need any more reminders of the woman who had stolen Quentin's heart. "I have assignments to work on this afternoon."

Quentin didn't argue, for which Amy was thankful. She hated feeling jealous of a woman who was no longer alive, but she felt it just the same and an uncomfortable silence developed between her and Quentin.

Did he know what she was thinking?

She was relieved when Shayna returned to the table with a small container of sauce and broke the tension. Shayna lifted the cheese with her fork and poured the sauce onto the dough, then went back for more and proceeded to use it as a dip for the pizza. Quentin fussed about her table manners, but Amy laughed and told him she was used to it. She'd had her share of supervising the lunch room when she taught first grade.

By the time they finished eating, Amy was stuffed and ready for a nap. Though she didn't relish the thought of the walk home, she turned down Quentin's offer of a ride.

"I need to walk off this pizza," she said. "I'm not used to eating so much."

"So we'll see you tonight then?" The look in his eyes was hopeful, and Amy glanced away.

"Please, Miss Welsh?" Shayna grabbed her hand. "You'll enjoy it. I promise."

"Yes, Miss Welsh." Quentin's tone was soft. "You'll enjoy it. I promise, too."

She glanced up then, and her gaze collided with his. Feeling her defenses crumble, Amy finally nodded.

"Good. We'll pick you up at quarter to six."

"No need. I'll meet you there." Amy would drive herself, leave herself, and that would be that. Riding to church together would be too intimate. Something she had to avoid at all costs. It would be much too easy to fall for Quentin Macmillan all over again.

And that was something Amy vowed would never happen.

8

Nerves hammered her stomach as Amy nosed her car into a space in the church parking lot. *Really, Amy, you're acting like an idiot. What do you have to be nervous about?*

It had to be the thought of being welcomed by strangers, being expected to tell a little about herself. Either that or being totally ignored. She didn't know which was worse, but right now she'd rather be ignored than be pressed to make small talk. Yes, that was it. That explained her jitters. This certainly wasn't about seeing Quentin again. The pizza this afternoon had been a pleasant surprise and had gone a long way toward easing her nerves where he was concerned.

No it hadn't. She was lying to herself. The thought of sitting nice and cozy beside Quentin on a church bench was far more nerve-wracking than entering a new church building for the first time. Quentin was a danger to her. She was on the brink of falling for him all over again and just as soon as she did...*boom.* He'd drop her before she knew what hit her. So why had she agreed to come? Because of those eyes. She knew it as well as she knew her birthday. One look into those sparkling blue depths and she managed to turn into a blob of Jell-O. It never failed. She was hopeless.

So...she glanced around the parking lot...where was Quentin anyway? Maybe he'd already rethought this whole thing and wasn't coming. It was no more than she should have expected from him. He was good at not showing up.

Leaning back in her seat, Amy closed her eyes and prayed for the courage to enter the building full of strangers. A knock at the window startled her and she jumped. Shayna. Quentin had kept his word after all. She felt inexplicably pleased.

"Hi, Shayna." She rolled down the window. "I didn't see your dad's truck, so didn't think you were here yet."

"We parked on the other side of the fellowship hall. Dad has to do youth group tonight, after all."

Youth group. That meant she'd have to go in to worship all alone. She fought down the full-fledged panic that had her wanting to tear out of the parking lot. She could get through this.

"It's OK, Miss Welsh. Dad said I could skip it to sit with you."

He'd thought of her. She was touched. He'd actually thought about how nervous she was over facing a group of strangers for the first time. She smiled over at Shayna.

"No, Shayna. I appreciate the thought. But I can manage on my own."

"Well...my dad did say you could join us in the fellowship hall if you prefer. The youth group leads children's church during the evening service. It's kind of fun. You might like it."

"I guess I have a decision to make, don't I?" She was more comfortable with kids than adults, and Shayna's expression was so hopeful, the decision was easy. "Let's go to children's church." Amy could tell by Shayna's wide smile she'd made the right decision. She rolled up the car window, gathered her things, and together they headed toward the fellowship hall. This would be a good way to ease into the church. Start with the kids, and then gradually feel comfortable with the adults.

"Amy." Quentin greeted her as she stepped into the large chilly room. He was standing in the center of the room behind a table scattered with papers. Behind him was a puppet stage. The room was filled with kids of all ages. "I'm glad you decided to join us. This was a last-minute thing. Russ couldn't come tonight. His wife is sick."

It had only been a few hours ago that she'd eaten pizza with him, but she couldn't believe the warmth that rushed through her when he smiled at her.

"Have a seat over there. I'm just making last minute preparations."

"I'll sit with you, Miss Welsh."

Amy followed Shayna to the back of the crowd of younger kids. She sat in one of the folding chairs, not far from a group of teenagers, and shivered as her rear made contact with the cold metal.

"I know it's cold. I've sent one of the guys to turn on the furnace. Pretty soon it'll be so warm in here we'll have to open the windows. Had I known earlier that I'd be taking over for Russ, I'd have made sure it was done in plenty of time for class."

"Hey, Macmillan."

"Shayna!"

The voices came simultaneously. A man and a tiny little girl with curly black ringlets. The man, taller than Quentin by at least five inches, with sandy brown hair, set the toddler on the ground and she ran with outstretched arms toward Shayna with all the might her chubby little legs would allow. Amy noted the pleasure on Shayna's face as she scooped the child into her arms.

"St. Nick." Quentin greeted the man with a handshake. "Hey, I'm glad you brought Emily. Shayna was chomping at the bit, waiting for you to show up."

"And Emily couldn't wait to get here." The man walked over to his daughter and kissed her on the cheek. "You have fun, sweetie. Daddy will see you later." He glanced at Amy with interest.

"Hello." She smiled, not wanting to appear rude by saying nothing.

"And who is this? Where have you been hiding her, Macmillan?"

"This is Amy Welsh." Quentin came up behind St. Nick, his tone chilly. "Amy, this is Nick St. James and his daughter, Emily."

"Hi, Emily." Amy greeted the toddler with a smile.

"Nice to meet you, Amy." Nick's smile lit up his face, and his warm voice sounded sincere. "Are you new in town?"

"Yes. I'm teaching at the high school."

"She lives down the road from you," Shayna burst in. Almost as soon as she spoke, a look of regret crossed her face. Amy couldn't help but wonder how Shayna knew where she lived. More importantly, why did she now look as if she'd given away some prized secret?

"Nick owns a tree farm beyond the woods that are behind the lagoon on Madrona Cove."

"Christmas trees?" The lagoon was just down the road from the house Amy rented, and she never noticed a tree farm. "They must be well hidden," she said.

"Yep. You can see the house and the lagoon, but the tree farm isn't visible from the road." Nick's grin was wide. "So you're the one renting the Kincaid place. How do you like it?"

"We need to get started." Quentin herded Nick toward the door. "Shayna will bring Emily to you after class." In a matter of seconds he'd managed to usher Nick out the door, but not before Nick looked over his shoulder and flashed Amy a huge smile. Quentin practically slammed the door in his face.

He was jealous. She rather liked that.

Quentin avoided her watchful gaze as he made his way to the front of the group.

"All right, you kiddos. Are you ready to sing?"

Noisy shouts went up, and Quentin raised his voice in a husky bass that sent shivers of pleasure dancing up her spine as he led the kids in a song about Noah building the ark.

The hour Amy spent with Quentin and the children was pleasant and passed quickly, an hour she'd gladly live through again. Quentin served as an MC of sorts, often leading the children in song, introducing the puppets and storytellers, and leading a prayer. She was in total awe of his interaction with both the young kids and the teenagers. He was a natural. And to Amy's delight, while the puppets were doing their thing, Quentin came and sat in the back with her like it was the most natural thing it the world for him to do—like he wanted her there for a reason other than the fact that his daughter had invited her.

The chairs were close enough together that when he first sat down his hard-muscled, denim-clad thigh brushed against hers. The touch, his denims against the thin cotton of her skirt, was so intimate and so deliciously thrilling, she wished she'd had on jeans instead. Perhaps then it would have merely been a thigh brushing a thigh instead of something that caused the pulse in her throat to leap wildly about.

Instead of apologizing as she'd expected, he flashed her a grin that reached his eyes and her heart. He stared at her with mischievous delight, then winked and turned his attention back to the front of the room. Amy was doused with a warm feeling of intimacy, a sense of belonging. Seventeen years seemed to melt away.

When class ended, several of the older kids ran out the door, either in search of their parents or to play on the playground. The spring days were growing longer, so there was plenty of light left. Most of the teenagers gathered in one corner of the room, talking and laughing loudly. Quentin did a great job of making sure the toddlers stayed put until their parents came after them. One parent in particular, Nick St. James, came as a surprise to Amy since Shayna had specifically said she'd take Emily to him. After retrieving his curly-haired daughter from a disappointed Shayna, Nick came over to where Amy stood observing as Quentin bid each child good night and warmly asked them to be sure to come back next week.

"It was nice meeting you, Amy." Nick held his hand out to her, and she shook it obligingly. "I hope you'll come back again next week."

"Yes, well I hope so, too. I'll have to wait and see." When he didn't let go of her hand, she gently tugged on it and added, "It was nice meeting you, too." Out of the corner of her eye, she saw Quentin approach. If that fierce scowl was any indication, he was not happy.

"Clear out, St. James. I need to get the rest of these kids off to their parents." The fact that he called his friend 'St. James' instead of 'St. Nick' did not escape Amy.

Nick blinked, clearly surprised at Quentin's rude growl, and shifted baby Emily on his hip. Giving Amy a last sweeping gaze with those perfect green eyes, he left the building.

Beside her, Quentin folded his arms across his chest, pushed out his lower lip, and tapped his right foot.

"What was that all about?"

"He was in the middle of a divorce and an ugly custody hearing when his wife suddenly died. He's not ready to get involved."

"Who said anything about getting involved? The man was just being polite." Amy couldn't believe the way he was acting. Territorial. Definitely jealous.

"I saw the look in his eyes. Believe me, it was more than polite. He's not the one for you."

Amy laughed at his audacity. "Don't you think you ought to leave that to me to decide?"

Quentin raked his hand through his hair and shifted his stance. "Look, I'm sorry. I overstepped my bounds. I didn't mean to."

Skeptical, Amy said nothing.

"Forgive me?" Raising one eyebrow, he stared at her, his crystal blue gaze unwavering. His mouth quirked up in one corner.

That's when Amy's heart warmed, and she had to turn away to refrain from stepping into his arms.

Across the room, Shayna was kneeling down laughing with a couple of little boys. Amy saw it as the perfect diversion.

"She's a good kid, Quentin. You've done a great job with her."

"Thank you." His eyes brightened and his smile grew wide as he pulled back his shoulders.

Amy could see the pride he felt and that pleased her. Quentin was good with teenagers, good with little kids. He was a great father. It wasn't hard to imagine him as a young dad swinging his daughter in the air, holding her on his hip much like Nick with Emily. She wondered if he'd been as good a husband as he was a dad.

"Amy?"

Amy blinked and realized Quentin had said something she hadn't even heard.

"I'm sorry. What did you say?"

"Where were you just now?"

"Just thinking," she murmured.

"I said I was sorry for the way I behaved with Nick. Forgive me?"

Unable to speak, she nodded. By now her heart was so filled with warmth toward him, she was helpless to deny him anything. Still, she had to say something so he didn't get the wrong idea and think she was putty in his hands.

"Don't do it again though. My life is my own and I won't have you interfering. Got it?"

Chagrined, Quentin nodded. Amy looked down at the floor and smiled. He was so easily manipulated by the females in his life. Or was she the one who'd just been manipulated?

Then the import of her previous thought struck her. *The females in his life.* Is that what she wanted to be? There was a glimmer of emotion that she quashed before it could be identified.

"I have to go now," she said quickly. "I enjoyed the evening though. You're a natural with these kids."

"Amy, before you leave I— the youth group meets for another hour. If you want to hang around we could go for pie and coffee after."

She wanted to. Honest she did. But clearly this was something she'd be better off avoiding. She glanced around to see what the teenagers made of their leader asking a woman out. To her relief, no one was paying attention—though Shayna appeared to be holding herself unnaturally still.

"I don't think so, Quentin. Thanks, though." She wasn't supposed to *want* to be around him anymore. She was supposed to get him out of her system, put the past behind her so she could walk away from Goose Bay with no regrets.

"I understand." Quiet disappointment darkened his eyes. Why? He couldn't possibly be interested in her again.

Amazingly, she found her voice. "Good night then."

"Yeah, good night." He said nothing else, and she turned away. "Amy, wait."

Hopeful, confused, she turned around. They watched each other in silence before he finally spoke.

"I'll walk you to your car."

"What about your class?"

"They'll be fine for a few minutes. I mean, look around you. They're a long way from getting settled." He was right. The kids were rowdy, laughing, and clowning around, and the last of the little kids had been claimed by their parents.

"All right. You can walk with me."

They walked in awkward silence, and Amy was

torn between relief and regret when they reached the parking lot. "Thanks again, Quentin." She opened her car door and stepped in.

"I'll give you a call."

"Good night."

He nodded and walked away, but not before she caught his sense of disappointment. She wanted to call him back, say "OK, I'll be expecting your call." But she didn't. Because she doubted he'd call. She had firsthand knowledge, inner scars to prove Quentin didn't always keep his word.

To take her mind off Quentin and all the turbulent feelings he inspired, Amy decided an aerobic workout was in order. She changed out of her skirt and sweater and slipped into a pair of sweats.

One of her goals, but not her sole purpose for coming back to Goose Bay, had been to see Quentin again so she could purge him from her thoughts. It was the only way she could move forward in her relationship with Jared. Now that she realized a relationship with Jared was out of the question, it should be simple. Get Quentin out of her system and leave town. Go home to Issaquah, and get on with her life.

She'd seen him, and she profusely thanked God, but Quentin was far from out of her system. What was she supposed to do now? Settling down on the plush champagne colored carpet, she inserted Lonestar's *From There to Here: Greatest Hits* into the CD player sitting on the floor in front of an antique cabinet where the TV was stored.

As Amy did her warm-ups and thought about the situation with Quentin, she began to pray, tuning out the sound of "Amazed."

"I don't understand, Father. I thought seeing Quentin again was the cure. See him, get over him, and move on. You answered my prayer. You let me see him again. You opened the door so I could come back here and deal with those feelings. Thank you for that. But what am I supposed to do now?

"His smile warms me up inside, watching him interact with the kids tonight was wonderful. I don't want to leave. I want to see more of him even though I know it's not the best thing for me."

How do you know it's not the best thing for you? The words whispered through her heart.

She just knew, that's all. Quentin had already broken her heart once. Her father had been right all those years ago when he'd called Quentin a loser and said he'd only hurt her. So how could staying here, seeing more of him, possibly be the best?

Trust Me. Let Me guide you. She could almost hear the words spoken out loud, wanted to believe them. Yet how did she know if they actually came from God, or if they were a product of her own wishful thinking?

Trust Me.

Faith. That's how she knew. Once she acknowledged that, an incredible sense of peace flowed through her.

She was on the floor doing stomach crunches to the beat of "You Walked In," remembering Quentin singing to the kids tonight and thinking how much he really did sound like Lonestar's Richie McDonald, when the phone rang. Instinct told her it was Quentin, and she was ashamed at how quick she was off the floor and across the room to snatch up the phone.

Realizing she should have turned the volume down *before* she answered the phone Amy raced, cordless in hand, across the carpeted room to the tape player. Unfortunately she cranked the volume up instead of down. The din was so disconcerting she almost dropped the phone trying to get the volume down.

"Sorry," she muttered, wondering if Quentin had any eardrums left.

"I see you haven't lost your penchant for Lonestar." He laughed in a way that tickled her ears. "At least I *think* that was them."

"Some music was meant to be played loud, Quentin." She wondered if he thought her less of a Christian for listening to non-Christian music. She didn't feel like explaining that she also liked Christian music. She just wasn't listening to it at the moment. That he recalled her habits after all these years, and worse, that he might be judging her for her musical taste, annoyed her for some curious reason. "What do you want?"

He was silent for a moment before answering. "Are you still angry at me over the Nick thing?" His voice was gentle, playing funny little games with her heart, confusing her all over again.

"No. Of course not." She sank to the floor and leaned against the side of the entertainment center. "I just—we can't do this."

"Do what?"

"See each other, talk with each other. We have a past, and there's no going back." The solace she'd found mere minutes ago faded as soon as she uttered the words.

"Why did you come back here, Amy?"

She swallowed hard. "I told you why. To fill in for Mrs. Baker." *To get you out of my system, out of my thoughts, out of my heart.*

"There's more you're not telling me."

"I wanted to check out the town. See if it was the same as I remembered." That sounded really lame, and she knew it.

"What are your plans after the school year is up? Are you going to stay on?"

"I don't know. Why are you asking me all these questions? We shouldn't even be talking to each other."

"Why not?"

He had her so discombobulated she didn't even know what she was saying. She leaned toward the couch and grabbed a throw pillow, then placed it behind her back.

"How was youth group?"

"Fine." He sounded pleased that she'd asked. "They came up with some new ideas for the children's church."

"They're really creative with the puppets and storytelling. I was impressed with the way they, and you, ran the children's church tonight. You seem to be a good influence on them."

"Thanks."

Talking on the phone with him reminded her of those long-ago nights they'd spent burning up the phone lines, whispering lovey-dovey talk to each other. She pulled the pillow from behind her back, threw it in the middle of the floor and lay down. "So what's this cool idea they came up with?"

"Did I say it was cool?"

"No." She laughed. "But your tone of voice did."

He joined her laughter with a low, rich rumble that rocketed through her. "You're right. It is cool, and

I'm excited about it. To a point."

She listened while he told her about the idea: a time machine. The kids would step through a door, one at a time. The door opened into a dark closeted space. A second door would open to a set constructed behind a partition. Backdrops would depict different Bible scenes. The youth group would dress up as Bible characters and let the children be active observers as the story was acted out.

"Quentin, that's a wonderful idea."

"Yeah." His response lacked his earlier enthusiasm.

"So what's wrong?"

"These kids are creative as far as storytelling and entertaining goes. But not a single one of them can draw a lick."

"So? Is there anything that says the backdrops have to be perfect?"

"Not as far as I'm concerned, but they want it to be perfect, or they don't want to do it at all. Amy, can we get together Friday night?"

The impatience with which he'd changed the subject startled her and she drew in a quick breath.

"There's something I want to discuss with you."

She couldn't see him again. She wanted to, but that wouldn't do anything to help her move on. "I'm busy that night."

"OK, Saturday."

"Quentin we have nothing to discuss. I've spied on your daughter for you. Something I don't intend to do anymore, by the way. She's a good kid, and I think both of us misinterpreted what she was up to. I'm quite sure she'll be just fine. So there's really nothing more for us to discuss. Unless—" She hesitated, unsure if she should even bring it up. "Unless you want to tell me why you never showed up that night."

Silence hung over the phone, heavy as the fog that frequented Goose Bay.

"I—can't. I don't want to discuss it. I—I've got to go now." Quentin's thick whisper was followed by a soft click.

He'd hung up.

No longer in the mood for Lonestar, Amy popped out the CD and spun it across the room like a Frisbee.

That fateful night seemed to have set the stage for every male relationship she'd formed since then—with the exception of Jared. He was reliable. He was dependable. He would never let her down. But Quentin would. Quentin had broken her heart once, and Amy was determined he wouldn't get a second chance.

9

"So, what's the scoop?"

At the sound of Miki's teasing voice, Amy looked up from her grade book. She took a sip of hot tea, orange spice, her favorite, before answering.

"There is no scoop."

"A date on Friday and church last night?" Miki tapped her short, neatly kept, maroon nails on the lunchroom table. "Sounds like you're in denial."

"It wasn't a date."

Miki raised one finely tweezed eyebrow. "Oh? What would you call it then?"

"It was a—" Amy sighed. She couldn't very well tell Miki the truth, thereby giving her a bad impression of Shayna. Nor could she admit to spying on one of her students. And she wouldn't lie and call it a date when it wasn't. "Just call it what you like," she groused. "I'm beginning to regret ever having come back to this town."

"I'm glad you're here." Miki pulled out the chair across from Amy and sat down, then reached out and touched Amy's hand. "I've been without a friend for quite some time."

"I know. Me, too." Amy picked up a plastic spoon and swirled it in her tea. "But there are things that make it complicated."

"Quentin." Miki's voice was soft and she nodded

her head as soon as she spoke, as if she knew she wasn't wrong.

Swallowing past the sudden lump in her throat, Amy nodded. Absently she watched the tiny whirlpool in her cup. Quentin. He complicated everything.

"I knew when I came back that I'd encounter him. I just didn't know when, and I certainly thought I'd be more prepared." She reached for a cube of sugar, plopped it in her cup, and watched it swirl until it dissolved. Then she laughed. "I'll tell you what. It's a good thing I didn't go to church with you the first few times you asked me. I definitely wouldn't have been prepared to walk in and see Quentin there."

Why didn't you tell me he went to the same church you kept inviting me to?

"It was bad enough," she continued, "that I had a student who looked just like him, who turned out to be his daughter. Bad enough." For the first time, Amy found herself sharing the details of Quentin's and her plans to run away and how he'd broken her heart, and that she'd come back after graduation to see if they could work things out.

Miki sighed sympathetically. "I know it was hard for you when you came back after graduation to find that he and Karen had just left on a delayed honeymoon. I honestly didn't realize at the time how brokenhearted you must have been. It didn't even occur to me that you didn't know he and Karen were married not long after you left town."

"I never saw it coming. Somehow I held on to the thought that he really loved me, that not showing up that night was something that couldn't be helped and that he'd wait for me."

Miki furrowed her brow in a thoughtful manner.

"You know, thinking back, it was kind of odd. They never dated. Quentin seemed lost without you."

That little piece of information gave Amy more satisfaction than she cared to admit.

"And then," Miki continued, "during Christmas break they just up and got married. It was supposed to be a secret ceremony, but word leaked out pretty fast."

"So I wonder why, if they never dated, he decided to marry her?"

"I don't know, but there was plenty of speculation. Speculation that never came to pass, if you get my meaning."

Amy did. It was a thought she'd had many times, but of course Shayna was much too young to have been the reason for the unexpected wedding.

"Then he joined the navy and they left town. He and Shayna only moved back after Karen died a couple of years ago."

The navy. This was the first she'd known that Quentin had joined the navy. It was also the first she'd known that he hadn't been in town all these years. But why the navy instead of following his dream of being a photo-journalist for *National Geographic* or some other wildlife society? And how did he end up in the construction business?

"Do you know what happened to Karen?"

"No, not really." Miki shook her head. "I heard it was some kind of cancer, but I never heard any details."

"I never really knew Karen." Even so, Amy felt sad that she'd died. "I knew she was Quentin's best friend, but that was as far as it went. She very rarely hung around Quentin when we were together."

"That might have been because she worked all the

time. During the school year, she had two part-time jobs. In summer, she usually had three. I don't ever remember anyone working as hard as Karen did."

This was news to Amy, and she felt sad that she'd never taken the time to get to know Karen well enough to know the burden she bore as a teenager. Of course Miki would have known. Miki had lived in town all her life and the locals seemed, at least back then, to know everything about everyone. Except for the reason Quentin married Karen.

"So Shayna lost her mother at one of the most important times of her life." Amy ducked her head so Miki couldn't see the moisture gathering in her eyes.

Having always been close to her mother, Amy couldn't imagine going through puberty and those turbulent teen years without her mother's presence. And Quentin. It couldn't have been easy for him, coping with the loss of his wife as well as having to deal with all his daughter's emotions. She felt such an overwhelming sense of compassion toward him; if he'd been in the room she would have thrown her arms around him.

And that's all it was. Compassion. Nothing else. At least, that's what Amy tried to convince herself as she took another sip of her now lukewarm tea.

Miki must have taken that as a sign that the conversation could continue. "They seemed so happy when they left town, it's such a tragedy that it ended up this way."

Of course Quentin was happy when he married Karen. Isn't everyone happy on their wedding day? Still, hearing Miki state the obvious stung, and Amy drew in a sharp breath.

"I'm sorry," Miki said. "I don't know why I said

that. I certainly didn't mean to be insensitive."

"It's OK." Amy knew Miki wasn't deliberately insensitive. Still, she decided to change the subject. "Tell me about Nick St. James."

Miki's mouth dropped open. "He's only the most gorgeous guy in town." She clasped her hand to her chest dramatically. "Those eyes!"

"Yes." Amy couldn't help but giggle. "Those green eyes. And those eyelashes."

"It should be a crime for a man to have lashes like that."

"It certainly should. But then, life's not always fair."

"No," Miki murmured, "it's not."

"Anyway, I met him last night. His little girl is a doll." Amy swore Miki's face brightened when she pulled her long dark hair over her shoulders and propped her elbows on the table.

Leaning forward, Miki asked in a conspiratorial whisper, "What do you want to know?"

"Quit looking at me like that. I don't want to gossip, I just want to know why Quentin called him St. Nick."

"He owns a tree farm outside of town. Not far from your place, actually."

"Yes, I know," Amy said impatiently. "Quentin told me that part. But I don't get the correlation."

"OK, it's cute, really." Miki straightened and grinned, the corners of her eyes lifting with delight. "Every year at Christmas, Nick has this little display. A Christmas village, I guess you could call it. He has hot cider and cookies and dresses up as Santa when the school kids visit. He even has a manger scene and straps hay bales on his neighbor's llamas so they'll look like camels. Kids love it. They look forward to it every year. I guess because of that, someone—I don't remember who—switched his name around and started calling him St. Nick instead of St. James. And it stuck. They even christened his tree farm St. Nick's Tree Farm."

Amy smiled. Curious about him, she'd driven past his place before coming to work this morning. Set back from the road in a grove of evergreens, the only identifying mark had been the sign announcing the tree farm.

"Hey, you're not interested in him, are you?" Miki looked concerned.

She shrugged and smiled nonchalantly. "He was very nice."

"And great looking."

But there was more to a man than looks. Amy certainly knew that well enough. "Are *you* interested in him?"

Miki flushed and glanced away.

That was all the answer Amy needed. "I have no plans to date Nick, Quentin, or anyone else. I only asked about Nick because I met him last night and was curious. But I won't deny he's gorgeous. So," she took a deep breath and changed the subject. "What's up in the drama department?"

"Just the usual. Rehearsals, costume design and fittings, temperamental leads, the usual slip-ups. Nothing out of the ordinary for this time of year."

Amy nodded absently. Miki was referring to the big end-of-year production everyone was looking forward to seeing.

"The one bright spot is Bradley Baxter."

Amy perked up, suddenly interested. "How so?"

"The kid is a whiz. He not only designed the entire set, he's constructed it as well. That kid has more talent than I've seen since I can't remember when."

That was all she needed to hear. Amy jumped up so quickly she almost upset her cup of tea.

"Excuse me, Miki. I have a phone call to make."

అం~

"I've got some news you're not going to like."

Quentin looked up from the house plans he was working on. Russ stood in the doorway, scowling, papers gripped in one hand. Whatever the news, it wasn't unusual to be interrupted several times a day with work-related problems. Quentin wasn't worried about that. It was Russ, and whatever was bothering him.

"What's up?"

"These were just faxed over. We lost the bid on the new bank."

A sick feeling stole over him, and Quentin forgot all about whatever was troubling Russ. He had a lot riding on this contract. This was the third major contract they'd been underbid on in the last month. Construction projects were in short supply, and he'd cut back wherever he could. But now it appeared he'd have to make the biggest, most painful cut of all. Staff.

"Any idea who the low bid was?"

Russ scanned the papers. "That same outfit from up north. Integrity Construction."

Quentin slammed his fist on the desk and stood up. "That's the third time they've underbid us. And our bid was ridiculously low. Check 'em out for me. Until the first contract they outbid us on, no one had ever heard of them. Find out whatever you can."

"Sure, Quentin," Russ obliged. "But what are we going to do in the meantime? The bakery renovation is almost finished, and we don't have any other projects in the wings."

"Relax, Russ." Quentin knew full well he had an entire work crew depending on him. He didn't need to be reminded of it. "I've got a project in the works. Let me do the worrying." Russ didn't look any more relaxed, but Quentin was reluctant to tell him more lest the condo project didn't come to fruition. If it didn't, he'd more than likely be ruined, taking his employees right along with him.

He'd been thinking about it for quite some time, and now that commercial construction was getting more and more competitive, it looked like the time might be right. He knew residential projects, even condos, were risky. But he'd done thorough research, and it appeared to be sound. It was best not to tell Russ about it yet, though, just in case the loan for the necessary property fell through.

"Whatever you're thinking about, Quent, I hope it doesn't go bust like these other projects have. Man, I can't afford to lose my job. Rusty will be starting college this fall, not to mention graduation and all those extra expenses. Plus Jennifer is getting married in July."

Pressure. Quentin didn't need it. Other people relying on him made him nervous. He didn't want anyone depending on him, didn't want to have to risk failing—letting them down.

"Things will be fine." He tried to assure his friend as well as himself. "I promise." If only he could be so sure. Business had been thriving three short months ago. Then he'd invested in new equipment, and now lost the third straight bid. Loans had to be paid, insurance, salaries. At this rate his business could go under before lunch.

"I have to get back to these plans, Russ."

Russ nodded but seemed reluctant to walk out the door. "Is that the new project you're thinking about?"

"Yes, but you can understand if I don't want to talk about it until it's firmed up. By the way, how's Janice?"

Shrugging, Russ gave a half-hearted smile. "She'll be OK, I guess." But he didn't look very convincing, nor did he sound as if he believed his own words. Was Janice sick? Is that why Russ seemed so upset and edgy lately?

"Is there something you're not telling me?" Of course Quentin knew there was, but maybe this was the opening to get Russ to talk about whatever was wrong.

Avoiding eye contact, Russ said, "Look, I've got to get back to work."

Certain now that something was really wrong at the Miller household, Quentin frowned. "OK. Check out Integrity for me, but don't worry. Everything will be fine." Maybe it was better not to push the issue right now. But he made a mental note to bring up the subject again. Soon.

"Russ," he called out before his friend disappeared down the hall. "If you ever need to talk about it, I'm here."

"Yeah, sure." Russ's muttered response left Quentin more puzzled than before. Whatever was bothering his friend, Russ wasn't about to spill it anytime soon.

Be with him, Lord. Help him through whatever the trouble is with his family.

"Quent?" Russ stuck his head through the doorway again. "You've got a phone call on line one. Louise says it's Amy Welsh."

Amy. He surprised even himself at how excited he was over the prospect of speaking with her again so soon. Maybe she changed her mind about Friday night. Only Russ's presence kept him from snatching the phone.

"Don't you have anything better to do?" Even though he snarled good-naturedly, he realized it was the wrong thing to do. A cloud seemed to wash over Russ's demeanor as he backed out the door.

Angry at himself, he buzzed the secretary before taking the call. "Louise, next time I have a call, tell me yourself."

"Amy, hi." He hoped his lousy mood didn't shine through in his tone.

"Bad day?"

So he'd failed. But just hearing the concern in her voice lifted his spirits.

"I'm sorry to bother you at work." Her voice broke through the silence. "I'll make it quick."

"No, don't worry. I'm glad for the diversion." Then a thought struck him. Shayna. He tried not to panic. "Is something wrong with Shayna?"

"No, no. She's fine. I don't even see her until the last class period of the day."

That was good then, he thought. But what wasn't good was the fact that he'd thought of Amy *before* he'd thought of his daughter. That rankled. His daughter was first in his life and always would be. No, he mentally corrected himself. God was. By putting the

Lord first, he would do right by his daughter and put nothing and no one but God before her.

"So what's up then?" He held his breath, hoping she'd changed her mind and was now willing to see him Friday.

"I just had an interesting conversation with Miki Loretta. She's the drama teacher. She told me about this whiz kid who designs and builds sets for all the plays." He could hear the excitement in her voice, imagine the smile playing on her face.

"I thought maybe you could use him with your youth group since you said you needed someone to design the time machine."

He really did need help designing the set. Not the structure of it, but the visuals, the murals, the desert scenes. The kids in the group were anxious to help pound nails and paint, but none of them—including himself—could draw worth a fig.

"Sure Amy. Who is it? I'll give him a call." He owed her big for this. He'd try again to talk her into going out on Friday.

"Bradley Baxter."

He wasn't prepared for her answer and his response was an immediate, deliberate growl. "No way."

"But Quentin—"

"No. No way. I'm not calling that kid for anything."

"But Quentin—"

"No buts, Amy. You don't know what you're asking."

"All I'm asking is for you to give him a chance. You need something and he can provide it. What better way for you to get to know him, to give him another chance?"

Quentin laughed. "I gave him a chance once. He's not getting another one. As far as I'm concerned, he's already proven himself."

"Quentin." Her voice was soft, wispy, and he didn't like what it did to him—commanding his attention, entreating him to listen to her. He steeled himself against her words, certain she meant to manipulate him into seeing things her way. No way. Not this time. "Maybe this is a chance for you to serve the Lord. Maybe *you* can provide something he needs."

He groaned and opened his mouth to protest, but Amy continued on with her one-sided dialogue.

"Can't you give him a second chance? You, more than anyone, should know how it feels to be prejudged."

That he did. She was right. Her father had prejudged him based upon his brothers and their reputations, as well as one little mistake on his part. Two, he reminded himself grimly. But that second one didn't come until after the fact and without the facts, it appeared to prove her father had been right about him all along. Just like Quentin was right about Baxter.

"No." He spoke louder this time.

Her disgusted sigh came through the phone loud and clear. Now was not the time to try and change her mind about Friday.

"You're making a big mistake."

"No, I'm preventing one." *Preventing the jerk from hurting my daughter the way I hurt you.*

"I don't believe you, Quentin. You teach Bible school, teach kids about love and forgiveness, teach them about Jesus. Yet at the same time you're refusing to reach out to a kid who perhaps has never had one bit of Bible teaching in his life. You have a chance to be an influence on him, to introduce him to the love of the Lord, and you're turning your back. Out of selfishness. Selfish because you're afraid he's going to replace you in your daughter's affections. I'm ashamed to even know you, Quentin. Don't call me again."

Stunned, he stared at the phone. She'd hung up before he could respond to her outrageous tirade. And in the process, Amy forgot one thing. She'd called him.

❧❧

Quentin couldn't believe Amy's outrageous suggestion that he ask Baxter to design the time machine for the children's church. What kind of idiot did she take him for? The guy was after his daughter, *and* she knew he'd had to fire the kid for harassing one of his other employees. She *knew* it. Yet she still had the audacity to suggest he put all that behind him and invite Baxter to be around Shayna more than he already was.

Not a chance.

"You have a chance to be an influence on him, to introduce him to the love of the Lord, and you're turning your back." Amy's words came back to taunt him.

She was right, of course, but influencing Baxter and throwing him together with his daughter were two different things. He could forgive the kid, but that didn't mean he had to like him, didn't mean he had to give him another chance.

The conversation had him so steamed he couldn't concentrate on work.

Amy's reminder about the way her father had

treated him hit a nerve. It wasn't a reminder he needed. Not now, not when his business was failing. Her father had been right all those times he'd said Quentin would never amount to anything, that he was a loser and would break Amy's heart.

"Louise, I'm taking off a couple of hours early. Russ can handle things here. I'll be at home if anyone needs me."

Louise cast him a puzzled look, but didn't say anything. She merely nodded as he walked out the door. He never took off early, never turned things over to Russ. He knew the building would be buzzing with speculations as soon as he left the parking lot.

The disagreement with Amy stayed with him on the drive home, but as soon as he parked the truck in front of his house, he discovered he had other problems. Glancing at the front door before he got out of the truck, he spotted the pink slip tacked to the door. He approached slowly, with wooden steps, knowing instinctively what it was. He read the wording with dismay.

City code #713a appendix c, states that farm animals may not be kept in the city limits. You are hereby ordered to remove the duck from these premises within seven days. If you choose not to comply with this order, the animal control officer will place the duck in the animal shelter for adoption. And in case you aren't aware, animals are only kept in our shelter for two weeks.

Crumpling the pink paper in his fist, Quentin groaned and glared across the lawn at Mrs. P.'s house. Lucky for him, she was nowhere in sight. He wanted to march right over there and...and what? He certainly couldn't attack a defenseless elderly woman. Nor would he, no matter how angry he was. But

Shayna...she would be so crushed. How would he tell her?

School let out at two o'clock, so he didn't have long to wait.

When she walked through the door at two-thirty, he still hadn't figured out a way to tell her.

"Dad, what are you doing home so early? What's wrong?"

Great. It was that obvious. "Sit down, sweetheart."

"Dad, you're scaring me."

"Oh, Shayna, no. It's nothing to be afraid of. It's just that you know how Mrs. Parsons is always complaining about Rufus?"

"Yeah, she's always threatening to call the police and have them take Rufus away."

"Well this time she's done it."

"No!" Shayna ran to the back door. Quentin saw her shoulders slump in relief when she saw the duck still in the yard. "Rufus." She pressed her nose to the window in the door, staring outside. "I won't give him up. I won't."

"Honey, if we don't find a home for him the city will come and take him away."

"It's not fair." She sobbed and flung herself into his arms. "It's just not fair."

"I know sweetheart, I know." Quentin held his daughter while she cried, all the while thinking mean thoughts toward his neighbor. It hurt...watching his child in pain. "We have until next Monday. I'll call Nick and see if he'll take Rufus."

"But we did that once before, remember? Rufus was miserable with Nick's ducks. They were mean to him. We can't put him back into that situation again."

"Shayna, we may not have a choice. We'll hold off

on Nick's until the last minute, but if we can't find anywhere else, then that's what it'll have to be. I know Nick will let you visit as often as you like."

"It won't be the same."

No, it wouldn't. His mornings with Rufus, silly as it may look to a casual observer, were important to him. He'd miss it. True he wouldn't hurt as much as his daughter, but he'd still miss the duck.

He shuddered to think what would happen if the animal shelter had to take him. Rufus would undoubtedly end up in someone's roasting pan. Probably that of his neighbor's. He was sure Mrs. P. and Foster would get great delight out of Roast-of-Rufus or Rufus Soup.

"What about Miss Welsh?"

"What about her?"

"She lives outside of the city limits. She lives in the old Kincaid place, and they have a huge yard. I bet she'd take Rufus for a while. Long enough for us to build a house in the country."

A house in the country? Is that what Shayna wanted? This was the first he'd heard of it. A dismal sense of failure coursed through him as he realized he wouldn't be able to give his daughter such a simple thing as a house in the country. If this house wasn't paid for, he'd be in danger of losing it as well as his business.

"Why don't you call her? She's probably home from school by now."

Somehow he doubted Amy would want to hear from him. Not after their last conversation.

"Come on, Dad, give her a call."

He took one look at the hopeful expression on Shayna's face and stepped toward the phone. He'd humble himself to Amy if he had to. Anything to keep that heartbroken look from his daughter's eyes.

10

There were three messages on her answering machine. All three were from Quentin, each one a bit more desperate than the last. Certainly not what she expected to hear when she pressed the button on the machine. She wasn't calling him back. There was nothing to say that hadn't already been said. Quentin Macmillan had an unforgiving heart.

So do you.

No, she didn't. She forgave easily and never held grudges.

What about Quentin? Aren't you holding a grudge against him?

No, she wasn't. She didn't hold a grudge. She was just protecting herself against getting hurt again. It wasn't the same thing at all.

Or was it?

How could he possibly hold a year-old indiscretion against Bradley? Didn't he realize a year was a very long time in the life of a teenager? Bradley's actions a year ago did not indicate the type of person he was today.

Intolerance and unforgiveness, as well as a lack of understanding, were all qualities Quentin had disliked about her father. She'd reminded him of that, but apparently it was something he chose not to remember.

She couldn't believe she could fall in love with someone so unforgiving. Of course, she wasn't *in* love with Quentin. She wasn't a kid anymore. She wasn't the same person who had loved Quentin, and he definitely wasn't the same person she'd loved. Half a lifetime had passed and now that Amy finally understood it, she could get on with her life.

That's why she was poring over ads, applications, and updating her resume. It was time to get next year's teaching position lined up, and it wouldn't be in Goose Bay. She circled two. One, a teaching position at a high school in Bellevue. The other, a tutoring job for a family in Forks.

Nothing had been accomplished by coming here. Her purpose for coming to Goose Bay at all, to try and settle the past so she could get on with her life, was at a dead-end. She'd failed. She probably would never be able to move on since she still didn't know why Quentin had stood her up that night. She would never know. Worse, she might not ever be able to put him out of her heart and fall in love with a man who was everything she'd always imagined Quentin to be. And that, quite possibly, was the biggest disappointment of all.

There was no place for her here and there never would be. Not until this very moment had she realized just how much she'd been hoping Quentin would confess his reasons to her and they'd walk off into the sunset to live happily ever after.

∂∘৩

Amy hated to admit to herself that she was disappointed when she checked her mailbox at school the next day and there were no messages from Quentin. Sometime in the middle of the night she'd had a stray thought that his message may have been about Shayna. If it had, then he would have left a message here. Which meant he wanted to talk to her for personal reasons. And she didn't want to talk to him.

When Shayna walked into class that afternoon Amy noticed the dark circles under her eyes. Her complexion was pale. Something was wrong. Perhaps Shayna really *was* the reason Quentin had called. Though curious, she refrained from asking even as Shayna came up to Amy's desk. "Please call my dad, Miss Welsh. He tried to call you several times yesterday."

"Is something wrong?"

"Yes, but I don't want to talk about it at school." Shayna bit her lip and the glint of unshed tears shone bright in her eyes. "Just call my dad. Please?"

Why hadn't Amy stopped to think something might be wrong? What made her conceited enough to think he'd be calling her for anything personal after the way she'd spoken to him last night.

"All right, Shayna. Since it's an emergency, I'll call him."

"Oh it's not an emergency like that." Shayna immediately looked as if she wished she could call back the words.

Amy shook her head, puzzled by Shayna's games. Was it, or was it not, an emergency? "I don't know, Shayna. Your father and I have nothing further to discuss. And you're my student. I shouldn't even be talking about this with you. Take your seat."

"It's not about your argument. It's something else. I promise. Please call him."

Shayna looked so dejected. Amy immediately felt

she'd been too harsh. At the same time, she was curious about how Shayna knew about the argument. Had Quentin been talking about her? Should she be flattered or offended? More likely, Shayna knew just because she was the kind of girl who kept an eye on everything to do with her father. "Shayna, I'll think about calling him, OK?"

Shayna's half-hearted smile was all the answer she needed. Something was really wrong, and it appeared she'd said just the right thing to give Shayna hope. When class was over, Shayna again begged Amy to call her dad. She didn't want to make the call in front of Shayna, so rather than use her cell, she started to head to the office to use the phone in there. But there still wouldn't be much privacy. Amy knew Quentin would still be at work when she got home, so she opted to wait until then since Shayna assured her it wasn't an emergency.

While walking back to the office to drop off some papers with the school secretary, Amy noticed Bradley and Shayna standing close together in the hallway by the lockers. She walked toward them feeling guilty for spying, but they looked much too cozy and she'd never be able to forgive herself if something untoward were to happen.

"I had a great time at the drive-in," Bradley said. "Maybe we should go again this weekend." Amy was close enough to see the suggestive look he gave Shayna, who bent her head and giggled. Quentin wouldn't like this one bit.

Oh come on Amy, she scolded herself. He's just being a kid. Here she was a teacher who always prided herself on understanding kids, reduced to spying on one of her students.

She deliberately focused on a couple of kids across the hall, determined not to eavesdrop on Shayna and Bradley. Still, the looks, the suggestive tones, the embarrassed sounding giggles when their heads were bent together had Amy worried. As soon as she walked in her front door, she called Quentin. His secretary said he was in a meeting. The woman asked to take a message in such an inquisitive, interested tone, Amy declined.

∂∾ઠ

As the week progressed, Amy noticed Shayna and Bradley spending even more time with their desks pulled together in the back corner of the classroom. As it should be, she told herself trying not to get too nervous about it. They were working together on a project, after all. She tried not to let herself notice the soft looks and flirtatious smiles they passed back and forth. But by Friday, the looks became more intense and her nervousness grew when Bradley threw his arm over Shayna's shoulders in a possessive and much too familiar manner. She really had to call Quentin.

All the way home from work, her nerves jumped. She hadn't spoken to him since that horrible conversation, yet she'd thought about him every single day. What would he think when she called him? Not that it mattered. Shayna was up to something. She was certain of it. And much to her dismay, she really did feel responsible.

She was barely in the door when she pulled her cell phone out of her bag. As she punched in the numbers she heard a startled cry.

"Ouch!" The male voice startled her.

"Is someone there?" The phone didn't even ring. The call must have connected at the same moment she flipped it open. "Hello, who's there?"

"Amy, is that you?"

Jared. Something in her froze. Her heart started thumping, and not in a good way. Once she'd made up her mind to call Jared and tell him they couldn't have a relationship, she'd allowed herself to get totally sidetracked. She'd never called him.

"Jared, hi."

"How are you, Amy?"

His voice was so tender, Amy felt ten times guiltier than she had before. Decent and caring, he deserved a woman who could truly love him with all her heart and soul. She just wasn't the one. She had to find a way to let him down easy. But how?

"Jared, I'm sorry I didn't call you back like I said I would. Things got out of hand." Her heart thumped heavy in her chest. Hurting him was going to hurt her, too. She prayed God would help her let Jared down easy. "Will you forgive me?"

"I missed you." He sounded so disillusioned, so sad. "When you first left, I thought I would go crazy with missing you."

"I'm sorry. It was something I had to do." She didn't want to hurt him further by repeating her reasons.

"I know, I know. You had to deal with your past before we could have a future."

Amy blinked, surprised. This didn't sound like Jared at all. The caring, the concern...they were no longer in his voice. "Jared, I—"

"It's OK, Amy. You don't have to say it." He seemed bitter. "So, have you?"

"H-have I what?" Amy swallowed hard, knowing exactly what he meant. What should she say?

"Dealt with your past. Made it right with that fellow you were always mooning over?"

So, she hadn't imagined the bitterness. It was real. And she was the cause. She never realized she'd been such a miserable failure when it came to concealing the hurts of her past. Obviously Jared read her better than she'd ever imagined. And it pained her that she'd hurt such a gentle man.

"Jared, I'm so sorry. I didn't think I was mooning over anyone. At least not that anyone else could see."

"Come on, Amy. Don't you think I'm smart enough to figure out why you could never commit to me?"

"Jared, I didn't realize—"

"I know you didn't." He sounded so angry. "You only thought of yourself, never about how your brooding and your moods affected me."

Was it true? Had she really been that selfish toward him? Shame washed over her. "I'm sorry. I never meant to hurt you. That's why I went away. So I could deal with this, so I could put it behind me and give you my whole heart."

"I don't want it."

"Please understand, Jared. Please?"

"I said," he lowered his voice and spoke slowly, "I don't want it."

"What?" Amy was confused. He didn't want what? Her explanation? Or...her heart?

Stunned, Amy stared at the phone. Then it dawned on her. When he said he'd missed her, it had been past tense. He didn't miss her anymore.

"There's someone else, isn't there?" Her not so

subtle inquiry was met with silence.

She waited.

The silence grew. Something inside her soared. Jared would be OK because he'd found a woman who could give him her whole self. *Thank you, God.* "It's OK, Jared. I understand. I can't expect you to sit around while I try to get my act together."

"I'm sorry, Amy. I didn't mean to sound so harsh." The bitterness was gone, but the guilt in his voice tore at her insides. Amy felt a piece of her heart chip off. This was her fault, not his. It was her fault this wonderful man was mired in guilt and bitterness.

"Jared, please." Amy spoke as gently as she could, wanting him to know she wasn't upset with him. In truth, she wished him every bit of happiness he deserved. "You didn't do anything wrong. I'm the one who is sorry. I'm the one who wronged you."

"No, you didn't. You thought you were over him. I don't think you'll ever be over him. Even though you were both young, something in your souls connected. You have to find a way, Amy. You belong together."

Tears blurred her vision and burned her eyes. "Whoever she is, Jared, she's a very lucky woman. I hope you'll be very happy."

"I hope the same thing for you, Amy."

Amy couldn't speak, so she gently closed her phone. When it rang again, a few minutes later, she wiped her eyes with the back of her hand before answering. "Jared, I'm sorry I hung up. I just— I couldn't—"

"Jared?"

"*Quentin?*" Amy's heart leaped as her stomach nose-dived. "Oh, Quentin, I thought you were someone else."

"Obviously."

He sounded...jealous. Impossible. Wasn't it? Her heart pounded.

"It's not what you think, Quentin. Jared is a— was a— friend. From Issaquah."

"*Friend?* Is that what you call it?"

Amy said nothing.

"Don't you return your calls, Amy?"

"I did return your call. You were in a meeting. And then, well, I just wasn't sure what to say after our last conversation. It didn't end well, if you remember."

"Of course, I remember." He sounded hurt.

"In fact, I was just getting ready to call you when Jared called. I need to talk to you."

"I need to talk to you, too. It's about Rufus."

"Rufus?" Who was Rufus?

"You know, Shayna's duck."

A duck? "Your urgent phone messages were because of a duck?" Amy wasn't sure if she should be offended or not. He wanted to talk to her about a duck. She needed to talk to him about his daughter.

"Yes, um...not just any duck. Listen, it feels silly discussing this over the phone. Can I come over?"

"No!" She definitely didn't want to be alone with him. It was too intimate. Her true feelings might betray her. It was better for them to meet in a public place. "Let's meet somewhere."

"Alfredo's?"

It figured that he'd pick their old hangout. But it had to be better than being alone with him here. "All right," she said with some misgiving. "Half an hour."

❧❦

Susan Diane Johnson

When Amy's metallic pink Honda Civic pulled
into the parking lot at Alfredo's, Quentin's heart
suddenly grew lighter. He jumped out of his truck to
greet her. As he approached the car, her smile took his
breath away. He didn't realize until that very moment
how eagerly he'd been watching for her. Nearly a week
had passed since he'd seen her, and all of a sudden it
seemed like forever.

"Amy, hi." Quentin hurried to open the door for
her, inhaling the fresh sunshiny fragrance of her hair as
she stepped out of the car. Her short-sleeved dress was
made of a white crinkly fabric with tiny flowers that
matched the color of her car. It was amazing the way
she looked and smelled so fresh after a long day at
school. He wanted to sweep her into his arms and see
if she felt as feminine as she looked.

"How'd you end up with a pink car?" He tried to
divert his thoughts.

"Mauve," she stated simply.

"I know my colors, Amy. I work with paint every
day. It's definitely pink."

"It's called Metallic Mauve," she insisted. "I have a
small jar of touch-up paint at home. I can show you the
jar and lot number if you'd like."

"I believe you, but I also know pink when I see it.
No self-respecting guy would ever drive a car that
color."

"Lucky for you," she looked over her shoulder
with a smile, "I'm not a guy."

"No kidding." Quentin bit back a smile, enjoying
the teasing, admiring the way the dress skimmed her
gentle curves. "What made you buy a car that color,
anyway?"

"Because it's the closest I could get to my favorite

152

color."

"Which is?"

"Pink." She tossed him another smile, and then pushed open the heavy wooden door.

They hadn't gone two feet when she stopped in her tracks, and Quentin walked right into her. "Sorry." She felt so good, so close. He inhaled deeply, reveling in her sweet fragrance.

"It's OK," she whispered. Instead of moving forward, she turned to look at him. Their faces almost touched and he found himself staring at her soft pink lips, remembering what they felt like against his. "Miki's here, and I don't want her to get the wrong idea about us."

"Should I be offended?" He said it jokingly, surprised to realize he was serious. But Amy's pleading smile was so disarming he found himself agreeing with her when she asked if they could get their food to go.

"We can go down to the beach and eat in either your manly truck or my girlie car."

As soon as she spoke the words, she seemed uncomfortable. She started to say something else, probably that she'd changed her mind, but was cut off by Miki shouting across the room.

"Amy, hi! Quentin Macmillan, is that you?"

"Oh, great." Amy gave Miki a half-hearted wave. "Don't encourage her." She spoke the warning under her breath as she stepped toward the tiny, dark-haired woman.

A nerdy looking man sat next to her, so close there was no denying they were on a date. Funny, he didn't seem the sort to be out with a woman like Miki.

"Stewart," Amy said pleasantly. "It's nice to see

you. Quentin, this is Stewart Snyder, the photography teacher at the high school."

Quentin shook the sweaty palm Stewart extended and hoped they wouldn't stick around for small talk. No matter the reason they were really meeting tonight, Quentin wanted Amy to himself.

Amy ushered Miki from the table, obviously so they could speak in private. She was probably going to warn Miki against giving him the third degree.

"I didn't know you and Stewart were dating." She spoke to Miki in what she obviously thought was a whisper, but Quentin could hear every word. "Be careful. I don't care how nice he is, no man can be trusted."

Though uncomfortable with Amy's comments, Quentin didn't want to discuss it in front of Miki. When the women returned to the table, he and Amy sat in strained silence, at the same table as Miki and Stewart, making small talk about things like the weather, while waiting for the pizza.

No man can be trusted. Obviously he was included in that comment. He knew what he'd done to hurt her. But who else had hurt her, and how bad? He hated that he'd hurt her, no matter how young and inexperienced he'd been. But even more, he hated that someone else had heaped hurt on her heart. Amy didn't deserve it.

11

When the pizza was ready they climbed into Quentin's truck and drove to the beach in an uncomfortable silence. The bay at the center of town was commonly known as City Beach. A dumb name, Amy thought, certainly not very imaginative in a town with a name as lovely as Goose Bay. But City Beach was far from commonplace. The crescent-shaped bay had the best view in town: tree covered bluffs, Mount Rainier on a clear day, small islands off in the distance, and, of course, water as far as the eye could see.

Sunset on a night like this was gorgeous. On the other side of town, just about a mile in the almost-opposite direction, you could look to the right and see the Cascade Mountains, then to the left and see the Olympics. Tonight the sunset behind them cast hues ahead, while the moon was already high in the sky. Strategically placed buoys intermittently flashed red and green lights. Remnants of an old wharf rose out of the water. During the day an eagle was often perched on one of the pylons.

After parking the truck in front of the driftwood-lined shore, Quentin took the pizza box from Amy's lap and flipped it open.

"I'm starved." He sounded as awkward as she felt.

Flirting with him earlier had been fun, and Amy regretted ruining it with her awful comment to Miki. Quentin obviously overheard her. She knew she should apologize, but she just couldn't. To do so would mean she'd have to explain. That would mean opening her heart and then she would be vulnerable to him all over again.

"Amy, the reason I called earlier. . ." Quentin hesitated.

"You mean the duck?"

"Rufus. We've had him for a long time. Ever since Karen died, actually. I know he's just a duck, but Shayna is about as attached to him as any other kid would be to their dog."

Amy sighed and thought back on how she'd always longed for a dog, a cat, a pet of any kind. Because they moved so often, she'd never been allowed to even have a hamster.

Quentin had grown quiet and stared out his window as the sunset shimmered on the gently rippling water. A couple drifted by on a paddle-boat, directly into the wash of moonlight.

Something was bothering him.

"Quentin, is something wrong with Shayna's duck?"

"Nothing's wrong with the duck. But one of our neighbors has decided to take a dislike to him and complained to the city. They've decided to enforce some code that prohibits farm animals in the city."

"But a duck isn't a farm animal."

"The city doesn't look at it that way. To them Rufus is a farm animal and if we don't get rid of him, they will."

A strange certainty was building in the pit of Amy's stomach.

"Amy, would you take Rufus?"

"Quentin, I don't know. I've never—"

"It's not hard. We'll come over and teach you what to do. All he needs is fresh water, cracked corn, and a little lettuce every day. Oh, and spaghetti if you ever have leftovers."

She was single. She always had leftovers.

"But Quentin, I live in the city. Why is it OK for me and not for you?"

"Technically you're just outside city limits. They can't enforce the code on you."

"What about your other friends?"

Quentin shook his head.

"We went through something like this once before. With the same neighbor. Only she didn't go as far as calling the city. She just complained a lot. We gave Rufus to the only person we could find. Nick St. James. You met him at church."

Amy remembered. The handsome single father with the adorable toddler.

"His ducks were merciless to Rufus. The poor little guy was miserable, and Shayna cried every time we visited him. Please, Amy?" Quentin took her hand and gazed into her eyes.

"How am I supposed to say no to that?" She was about to get that pet she always wanted.

He smiled at her, the blue of his eyes deepening. He leaned close. Amy held her breath while she waited for him to kiss her.

Something cracked against the windshield and startled them apart. They both looked at the window in alarm. A seagull sat there staring at them.

"Nasty seagulls," Quentin muttered. "Get off my truck."

Amy burst out laughing. "I think he wants our food."

She picked up a slice of pizza and sure enough, the scavenger's beady eyes followed every movement she made. She started to open the window and the gull opened his beak wide enough she could almost see into his gullet. The sound he made was horrible.

"Gross!" Amy squeezed her eyes shut. "I can't stand looking at him while he makes that awful sound. It's hideous."

"What's hideous? The sound or the inside of his throat?"

"Both!"

"I agree. Don't throw the pizza out until we're leaving. Otherwise all the friends he just called will make a mess all over my truck."

Just as Quentin pulled away from the beach Amy tossed a slice through the window. Sure enough, two-dozen gray-and-white gluttons descended on the ground and began pulling at the piece of pizza.

"They'd gobble this entire pizza in seconds flat if we gave it to them," Quentin said.

"But don't waste it like that. Take it home to share with Shayna."

"Can't."

"Why not?"

"She's not home. She's spending the night with Ashley."

Unable to help herself, Amy sucked in a breath.

"What?"

Avoiding Quentin's question, she leaned back in her seat. "I was afraid of that." Her stomach headed into a free-fall.

"Why? What's going on?" Quentin pulled the truck over with a jerk of the wheel and came to an abrupt halt.

"I think the girls are planning something again."

"You mean with Baxter?"

She heard the anger in Quentin's tone. "Bradley," she corrected softly. "His name is Bradley."

"I know what his name is," Quentin snapped. "I prefer Baxter."

Amy knew Quentin was just doing what he felt he must. A father bear protecting his girl cub.

"I've seen these growing looks between them all week long, and I've been concerned. I'm certain they're up to something again."

"Why didn't you let me know this sooner?"

She shut her eyes against the anger in his tone. She deserved it. He was right. She should have said something sooner.

"I— I wasn't totally sure. I thought maybe they were just working on their assignments."

"You and their assignments. If you hadn't assigned them to work together in the first place, none of this would be happening."

"Quentin, I've explained this to you before. I had no idea before I paired them up. Once I knew, I couldn't very well separate them."

"You could have, you just didn't want the hassle."

"That's not true. I'd do anything for my students if I thought it was the right thing. You may not remember this, but if you tell a girl she can't see a certain boy, what will happen?"

That Quentin was silent spoke volumes to Amy. She knew he was remembering when they were teenagers.

"Amy?" His voice softened. Amy sensed he had a difficult time reining in his temper *and* his fatherly emotions. "Will you help me?"

"Of course I will, Quentin. But what can we do? We don't know for certain they even have anything planned. It's just my suspicion."

"Since she's already headed over to Ashley's for the night, why don't we do a little stake out?"

"A stake out? You mean of Ashley's house? Like spy on them again? Follow them?" Great. She had a hard enough time spying on Shayna at school. Now he wanted her to do it on a larger scale.

"I was convinced it was just friend stuff." Worry showed in fine lines around Quentin's eyes.

"Friend stuff? What do you mean?"

"After Shayna and I talked about the drive-in escapade, she assured me Ashley's mom knew all about it, and it was simply guys and girls getting together. Just friend stuff. That's why I didn't worry any more about it."

"Oh." And here she'd been seeing signs all week, thinking he could handle it since he was aware of it. He was right. She should have let him know sooner. She really was responsible. And because of that, she had no choice but to agree. "OK, Quentin, I'll go with you to keep an eye on the girls. *But*, I don't like spying on people one bit. I hope this is the last time."

❦

Apprehension battled with joy in Amy's heart. More time with Quentin might be just what her heart wanted, but she knew it wasn't wise. She'd never get out of this town with her heart intact.

Sitting in the truck for over an hour, listening to an oldies station with Quentin brought back memories Amy knew weren't good for her.

Quentin must have been lost in memories, too, because he'd barely said two words since they'd pulled up in front of Ashley's house.

There'd been no sign of activity other than the flutter of curtains now and again, and Amy wondered out loud if perhaps she'd been wrong about Shayna and Bradley planning something.

"No, I'm sure you were right, but for some reason they changed their minds." His relief was clearly visible on his face.

Amy felt it, too. "I'm glad," she said.

"Me, too."

"But, Quentin, you know they'll probably plan something again."

He blew out a heavy breath, and Amy could almost see the thoughts swirling in his head. Her heart went out to him.

No parent wanted to think of their teenage girl out sneaking around with boys. But Quentin was having a terrible time with it. More terrible, she suspected, than most. She doubted it would be any different if the boy was a straight A student with perfect manners.

Quentin was having difficulty just thinking of his daughter growing up.

She wanted to reach out and touch his hand, to comfort him, to reassure him. But a sudden sense of shyness overtook her and she held back.

"It's probably safe for us to leave now."

Amy nodded, disappointed when Quentin started the truck. Too bad the night couldn't last forever. There was nothing she had ever wanted more than to simply be with Quentin. Now she was. And though she'd previously asked God to give her just one more glimpse of him and that would be enough, suddenly it wasn't.

As they neared the restaurant where her car was still parked, Amy recalled the awkward way their evening had begun. She had yet to apologize. She'd been about to when the issue with Shayna and Ashley had come up. Now, though, she simply must offer her apology.

"Quentin, I'm sorry."

"For?" Quentin stared straight ahead, watching the road.

"You know what for."

Quentin remained silent. He knew exactly what for, but he was going to make her say it. Nothing like adding to the humiliation.

"My crack to Miki about men."

"Why did you say it then?"

"Because it's true."

Quentin flinched as though she'd hit him.

"I'm sorry, Quentin, but it is. Every man I've ever loved or cared about has thrown my heart down and stomped on it. My father, Stevie Michaels, Jared, you." OK, throwing Jared in there wasn't really fair since he'd had every right to find someone who would cherish him.

"Stevie Michaels?" Quentin clenched his jaw.

"He was the boy I had my first crush on. It was back in grade school. I thought I loved him. I used to pray to God every night asking to marry him when I grew up."

She smiled at the silly childhood notion.

"He broke your heart?

Amy nodded.

"What did he do, the little punk?"

Could it be that maybe, just maybe, Quentin did

care about her? The thought warmed her insides.

"He took a note I'd written him, and read it to the entire fifth and sixth grades and their families. We were at an assembly and kids were doing skits. Instead of a skit, Stevie read my note—complete with a high-pitched girlie voice. 'Dear Stevie, I like you. Do you like me? Yes or no? Love, Amy Welsh.' Everyone in the entire building laughed at me, and I wanted to die on the spot. Naturally, I didn't. I was teased mercilessly for weeks after that."

"I hope he grew up to marry an army drill sergeant who never cuts him any slack."

"You know, you almost described my dad. Except he was navy, not army."

"And they don't have drill sergeants in the navy."

"No, but my dad was close enough. He would have fit in the army just fine." She contemplated her next words carefully. "And then there was you, Quentin. Not only did you stomp on my heart, you shattered it."

Quentin shifted uncomfortably and looked in the rearview mirror before turning into the parking lot. After he parked, he took one hand off the wheel, reached across the seat and fumbled for Amy's hand.

"I'm sorry, Amy." The same warm tenderness she felt as his hand gently clasped hers was evident in the soft tone of his voice.

"You made it so I could never love anyone again." She felt seventeen again, felt the old hurt like a fist in the stomach. "Why, Quentin? Why did you leave me to sit in the dark for hours waiting for you to show up?"

He was quiet for an uncomfortably long minute before he looked at her with a steady blue gaze.

"So, didn't you love Jared?"

Amy fell back against the seat. That was it then. She wouldn't be getting any answers today—as usual. Quentin really excelled at avoidance where she was concerned.

"I cared about him, but I didn't love him."

"Then how could he have broken your heart?"

"Well, he—" How could she explain without revealing how she'd actually been the one to do the heart-breaking?

"Were you engaged to him?"

"No." Amy hesitated, still searching for the right words.

"Then what?"

"I don't know why I'm telling you this, but I did care about Jared. Not love. At least not *that* kind of love. Brotherly love. But by the time I realized it, he'd already asked me to marry him."

"And you said yes."

"No, I—" She sighed heavily. How much of her heart should she lay bare? "I told him there was something holding me back from committing, and I had to put it behind me first."

"Something...meaning me?"

She swallowed hard. Her cheeks burned. She looked at the door handle and considered opening it. A gentle touch on her shoulder stopped her. Before she realized it, Quentin's strong arms were wrapped around her and her face rested against his chest. She could hear the thumping of his heart, feel the rise and fall of his breathing.

"I'm so sorry, Amy. I wish you could know how sorry I am."

She couldn't say it was OK, because it wasn't. And she didn't want to sound bitter. So she said nothing.

"I'm the reason you came back, aren't I? And I'm the reason you didn't accept Jared's proposal."

"You know you are," Amy whispered into his chest, mortified to realize her tears were dampening his shirt. She pulled away and wiped her eyes.

"I'm sorry, Amy."

"I don't want your apologies, Quentin. I just want to know why."

"Amy, I— I can't."

She swallowed hard and nodded, then got out of the truck.

As she shut the door, she heard him whisper in a pain-filled voice, "If I told you why, you'd never forgive me."

12

Why had she agreed to keep the duck?

Amy paced the floor for the sixteenth time, the lump in her stomach growing with each footstep.

If Quentin and Shayna's duck lived with her, that would mean they'd come over to visit. How often would they be here? Weekly? Daily? And even if they didn't, the feathery creature would be a daily reminder of Quentin.

Why had she agreed to keep him?

It was only temporary. She had to remember that. She wouldn't be in Goose Bay much longer. When school let out for the year, she would move on. But even that didn't matter. Any further ties with Quentin Macmillan would be destructive to her heart. And Rufus was tied directly to Quentin.

She was an idiot. She had to call and tell him to forget it. He'd have to find some other duck-sitter.

Tires crunched the gravel in the driveway, followed by the slamming of one vehicle door after by another.

They were here.

Too late to back out now.

No, it wasn't. She'd just do it face to face.

She flung the door open, and her heart jumped.

Quentin was in the yard, walking backwards. A huge smile lit his face as he coaxed a duck toward the fenced backyard with a piece of lettuce. The duck was precious with his dark green head and grayish brown body. Simply adorable. If she didn't take him, Shayna and Quentin would lose a pet they so obviously adored. Worse, Rufus might end up being euthanized by the city.

Shayna stood next to the truck watching her father, her smile almost as wide as his, a contrasting mixture of exuberant child and maturing young woman, each warring for a foothold in both her body and soul.

Amy felt her heart catch in what could only be described as a maternal tug.

At that very moment, she wanted to take Shayna in her arms and be the mother Shayna no longer had— to tell her it was OK to be herself and enjoy the simple things of life. She didn't have to grow up as fast as her peers dictated.

"What do you think, Miss Welsh?"

Amy smiled. "I hope I can make him happy."

"You will." Shayna nodded, full of enthusiasm. "It's easy. Just feed him in the morning and put him in the pen at night so the raccoons don't get him. Oh and make sure he has fresh water, too."

Raccoons? Amy felt even less sure than she had earlier. "Wait a minute. I don't have a pen."

"You will, soon." Finished playing with the duck for the moment, Quentin walked over to where they stood.

"I will?"

"Dad's going to build one." Shayna grabbed Quentin's arm and leaned against him.

Quentin positively beamed. These two had such an obviously wonderful relationship. They must have been quite the happy family. Quentin, Karen, and

Shayna. A terrible twinge of jealousy gnawed at Amy's insides. She felt unsettled, distressed, an envious outsider looking in.

What would it have been like if Shayna was her daughter and Quentin her husband? Would Shayna be as happy and well-adjusted with Amy for a mother? Would Amy and Quentin still be married? She'd heard more than half of all teen marriages ended in divorce.

No. Amy was quite sure she and Quentin would have made a marriage work. He'd made one work with Karen, after all.

Why are you dwelling on the past, Amy? Don't waste your time that way.

Amy blinked. Where had that thought come from? No matter how badly she wanted to listen to the words the Lord whispered in her heart, Amy knew one thing. It was easier said than done.

Father, God, I don't want to dwell on the past. Please help me put it behind me so I can get on with my life. And Lord, please help me figure out exactly what it is I want and where it fits in Your will.

If it is with Quentin, Lord—and I'm so afraid that's what I really want—please don't let him hurt me again.

"Amy? Are you OK?"

Amy looked up, startled at the sound of Quentin's voice. She saw concern line the corners of his eyes and her heart tripped.

She sighed deeply, and then smiled at him. "Sorry, Quentin, I was just lost in thought. So, we're going to build a duck pen?"

He slapped the side of the truck and for the first time, Amy noticed a roll of chicken wire, a neat stack of two-by-fours, and a plastic swimming pool.

"I'm going to build it. You've done enough by

taking him in. Actually," he lowered his voice so Shayna couldn't hear. "I'd like it very much if you hung out with me while I work."

Again, her heart tripped.

"OK, but will you at least let me haul some of the wood?"

"No can do." Quentin shook his head, reaching for Amy's hands. He caressed them with his, his eyes never leaving hers. "We don't want any slivers marring up these pretty hands of yours."

Amy felt the blush burn her cheeks and noticed Shayna watching them with interest. She needed a distraction.

"Why the swimming pool?"

"For Rufus to swim in. Don't change the subject."

Gently, she extracted her hands from his. "How about if I bring you and Shayna some iced tea? I'll be right back."

Clearly, the attraction between them wasn't about to disappear. Amy had to work on trust issues with Quentin, but she felt her heart filling with a sense of hope. Was it really possible for them to bury the past?

Lord, is being with Quentin Your plan for me? If it is, I trust You to work it all out.

Absently she reached for the pearl necklace hidden beneath her t-shirt, aching for her hopes to become reality.

ॐॐ

"Here you go." Amy placed a glass of iced tea on top of Quentin's toolbox.

He stared at her, swallowing hard. Even dressed in blue jeans and a lime green t-shirt, she was every inch a lady, and he ached to take her in his arms. Everything about this seemed so right—working in the yard, Amy bringing him something to drink with that wide kissable smile on her face. Just...being with her.

He reached for the tea and took a huge gulp, unable to keep his eyes off her. "Thanks."

"You're welcome." Amy held up another glass. "I brought one for Shayna, too. Where'd she go?"

"She went around to the side of the house with the duck. They're exploring the yard. This is a great place, Amy. I can't tell you how much I appreciate this."

"I'm glad to do it, Quentin. Shayna's a wonderful girl. I'd hate to see her lose her pet."

Quentin put his tea down and scooped his tape measure off the grass. "She is wonderful, but I'm worried about her."

"The Bradley thing again?" There was an edge to her tone that wasn't there a few minutes ago, unsettling Quentin.

"Partly." He hurried to explain. "She's growing up so fast. One minute she talks about Bradley and makeup and clothes, and the next she's out in the yard with the duck. But mostly she talks on the phone with her girlfriends and just doesn't have as much time for me as she used to."

"He cares for her, you know?" Amy's eyes were soft with concern, her voice gentle. She placed her arm on his.

Quentin set his lips in a grim line and stepped away from Amy, knowing he was acting childish. He knew Bradley cared for Shayna. He just didn't want to admit it. Nor did he want to think about what his daughter felt in return.

She was too young, and much too good for the

likes of him.

Oh, who was he kidding? No matter who the boy was, he'd undoubtedly feel the same way he felt right now. Like a father terrified of his daughter stepping too close to an adult world.

He looked back at Amy. She watched him, almost as if she held her breath. She watched him like she cared.

When she reached out and touched his hand, her bittersweet smile of understanding zinged his heart. She made him feel so good. She did wonderful things for his senses. He wanted her in his life. He would do whatever it took to keep her there.

Even if it means giving Bradley Baxter a chance?

The thought tripped him up for only a second. *Yes, Lord,* his heart answered. *With Your help, I will.*

What about telling Amy why you hurt her? Give her the answers she needs so you both can heal.

Drawing in a heavy breath, Quentin looked into Amy's compassion-filled eyes. His stomach plummeted. Would she look this concerned for his emotions after he told her the truth?

It's the only way.

OK, Lord. I trust You. I can do it, through You.

Dropping the tape measure back to the ground, he walked toward her. No time like the present to get started. The sooner things were in motion, the faster he could square things with Amy. He tucked his hand under her elbow and gently guided her toward the porch.

To her credit, Amy didn't argue. She simply followed his lead and sat with him on the cement steps.

His heart thumped with nerves as he wondered

how she would respond.

Trust me.

Eyes wide with curiosity, Amy searched his face. "Did you want to talk about something?"

He nodded his mouth suddenly dry. "Bradley."

Amy's mouth tightened.

"No, you don't understand," Quentin said in a rush. "I need you to call him for me. Set up a meeting so I can look at his artwork and we can talk about the mural. See if he's interested."

Amy's smile was instant, and he longed to trace it with his fingertips. But before he could act on his impulse, she acted on one of her own. She threw her arms around him, throwing him momentarily off balance. As he struggled to keep from falling backward, he squeezed her tight. It felt so natural, so right. He didn't want to let her go.

"Quentin, this is the absolute best news you could give me! How? Why?"

"The Lord, Amy. With a little help from you along the way, constantly pricking at my conscience about forgiveness. You're so right. I'm a Christian. How can I hold a grudge against a teenager who's trying to straighten out his life? It *is* about forgiveness, second chances. Not the past."

Amy sucked in a breath, an odd expression on her face. Before he could question her about it she composed herself, nodded, and started to rise from the steps.

"I'll call him right now."

"Just a minute." Quentin tugged her back down and her blue-jean clad leg brushed against his. "There's more."

"More?" Her eyes widened.

"Yes, and it concerns you." He took her hand, so tiny, so soft and feminine, in his. "You and me."

Amy bit her bottom lip and looked away.

"Amy." He reached out and traced her cheek with the back of his hand, then gently pulled her chin toward him so he could see her face. "It's time for us to talk."

Still avoiding his eyes, she nodded.

"Tonight."

Painfully slow, she lifted her gaze to meet his eyes. Her wounded look, mixed with hope and guilt, assaulted him. He alone was responsible for her pain. It pricked deeply into his conscience.

"Tonight?" Her whisper was one of caution. "You're really going to tell me?"

He ached to kiss her pain away. Instead, he nodded. "Let's get things clarified once and for all, so we can put it behind us and move forward."

"Oh, Quentin, that's all I want." Amy squeezed his hand, and he pulled her against him, her head resting on his chest. He brushed his cheek against the top of her head for a minute before she looked up at him.

"Thank you," she whispered.

Her lips were so near his, he did the only obvious thing—he dipped his mouth to hers, claiming a sweet, chaste kiss that had him longing for more.

Amy pulled away just as he started to deepen the kiss.

"What—?" Disappointed, he looked up.

"We have company." She pointed at the corner of the house where the hydrangea bushes were rustling back and forth.

"Shayna." He used a low, stern tone. A second later his darling daughter popped around the corner.

"Hi, Dad." She was positively beaming.

"I hope you weren't spying on us."

"Oh, no, not at all." Shayna bit her lip in what appeared to be an effort to keep from smiling. "Dad, can I cook dinner for you guys?"

"Dinner? It's barely past lunchtime. You can't possibly be hungry yet."

"I know, but I want to thank Miss Welsh for taking care of Rufus. And you, too, for building him a new pen."

"Are you sure, honey? That's a lot of work."

"Yes, I'm sure. I want to. Please?"

Unable to refuse his daughter when she looked so happy, Quentin turned to Amy.

"Please say yes. We'll have our talk then." He used the same pleading tone Shayna had, and the payoff was a shy nod from Amy.

After the pen was built and the mess cleaned up, Quentin filled the pool with cold water from the hose. Rufus waddled up the ramp and jumped in, contentedly gliding from side to side in smooth circles.

Quentin explained to Amy how important it was to make sure Rufus was safely locked in the pen each evening before dusk when the raccoons came out for the night. It wouldn't take long for one of them to kill the duck.

Amy looked nervous.

"What if he won't go in?"

"Don't worry," Quentin assured her. "Everything will be fine. Just walk behind him and he'll go right in."

"Dad, are you coming?" Shayna sat in the truck with the window down. "We need to go to the store to buy stuff for dinner. I want everything to be perfect."

"In a minute." He looked back at Amy. "I'll see you tonight, right?"

Amy nodded. "I'll be there."

A sudden sense of fear squeezed Quentin's insides. He'd tell her tonight, but what if she refused to forgive him. He didn't want this wonderful promise of new beginnings to be forever dashed on the rocks of broken dreams.

"Quentin, what's wrong?"

He pressed his lips together unsure what to say. How did he voice his fears without feeling and sounding like a loser?

"Come on. Tell me."

He sighed, opened his mouth to speak, and stopped.

"What?" Amy came closer to him, concern written on her face. She touched his upper arm. He wanted to sweep her into his arms, but resisted. "Quentin, tell me, or I won't eat with you tonight."

"You have to. You already agreed. You don't want to disappoint Shayna." He placed one hand over hers, where it still rested on his arm. "Or me."

"OK," she said in all seriousness. "I'll be there."

Relieved, he nodded and started toward the truck.

"Quentin," she said. "Don't worry that I won't forgive you. As long as you're honest with me, we can overcome the past."

"I hope you're right, Amy," he said to himself as he climbed into his truck. "I hope you're right."

Somehow, he doubted she would really forgive him when she learned the truth.

13

From the way Shayna set the picnic table, one would almost think this was a date.

Fat candles in old-fashioned jelly jars sat at either end of the table. The heat from the flames gave off a slight fragrance of cinnamon before drifting into the fresh air.

Paper plates and napkins in a deep burgundy color matched the candles and the flowered pattern in the table-cloth. A bouquet of spring flowers arranged in a vase and a deliciously crisp looking salad sat beside it. Shayna had obviously worked hard to impress her, and it worked.

"Shayna, everything looks beautiful."

"Thank you." Shayna, who was still arranging food on the table, blushed.

"No, thank *you*. It's been a long time since anyone has gone to so much trouble for me. Are you sure you don't want any help?"

"No, really, Miss Welsh. I want to do this. I—"

Something was wrong. Amy's teacher instincts were instantly alert. "What is it, Shayna?"

Shayna shook her head. "Nothing. I hope you and my dad enjoy the dinner."

"Of course we will." For the first time, Amy realized there were only two plates. "Aren't you eating with us?"

"Can't." Shayna shook her head. "Ashley and I

have plans."

"I'm sorry to hear that." Even though it meant she'd be alone with Quentin, which was a nice thought, Amy was disappointed. She enjoyed being around Shayna. But her teacher's instincts just kicked up another notch. "What are you girls going to do?"

"Nothing much." Shayna avoided Amy's eyes. A sure sign to beware of, Amy knew.

"Are you sure?"

Shayna looked up, a challenge in her blue eyes. "I'm not going to the drive-in again, if that's what you mean."

"OK." Amy wanted to feel relieved, but there was something in Shayna's expression that left her unsettled. "Just remember, lots of girls your age end up in unexpected circumstances when they do things that seem perfectly innocent."

"Don't worry about me, Miss Welsh. I know exactly what I'm doing." Shayna's expression changed, the challenge gone, and her eyes sparkled. "Come on, Dad," she called. "Time to eat."

Shayna placed a platter of hamburgers and a plate of oven-baked French fries on the picnic table.

"Something smells good." Quentin stepped out onto the porch and planted a kiss on his daughter's forehead. "Amy, you match the table setting." He gave her a half-smile that set her senses skittering.

She blushed under his scrutiny, pleased he'd noticed, and glanced down at the front of her dress to make sure all the buttons were properly in place. It was a short-sleeved ivory dress with buttons from collar to hem, delicately embroidered with flowers in shades from pink to burgundy.

"Have a seat, you guys. You don't want it to get

cold." Shayna ushered them into chairs she'd pulled outside from the dining room table. "Good night!"

Quentin reached out and grabbed her arm. "You're not staying?" He looked disappointed.

"Ashley and I have plans."

"Shayna." His tone was low, authoritative.

"Don't worry. I've already talked to Miss Welsh. Ashley and I are just going to watch TV, nothing more. Just the two of us. Nothing to worry about."

Quentin looked doubtful, unsure.

"Dad, I promise. We'll be fine and I won't get into any trouble."

"I don't know..."

"Dad, please?" Shayna's voice turned pleading. "I promise. Really and truly. We're not going anywhere. You can even call Mrs. Morgan and ask her yourself."

Amy watched the two of them with interest. Their affection for each other was obvious. Even if Karen were still alive, Amy suspected the bond would be deep. Shayna was her father's little girl, and always would be, and Amy was proved right as Quentin turned to putty in his daughter's hands.

"OK." Quentin tried to look stern but didn't quite make it. "Just be sure and be where you say, because I'm calling to check up on you. And there'd better be no boys over there."

Shayna nodded, looking pleased. She turned to go.

"Shayna, one last thing."

Rolling her eyes, but still smiling, she turned to her dad. "What?"

"Thanks for tonight. It's really special."

"Yes," Amy added. "Thank you."

If possible, Shayna's smile widened as she disappeared through the doorway.

"It looks to me like we've been set up."

Quentin looked surprised. "You think?"

"Oh, come on. Quentin, it's obvious."

"Yeah, I guess it is. I had no idea my daughter was a scheming little matchmaker."

"Now you do."

Reaching across the table to take Amy's hand, Quentin grinned. "She did well."

Amy ducked her head to hide the blush burning her cheeks. She'd come to town to get Quentin out of her heart, to put the overblown teenaged infatuation out of her soul once and for all. But being reminded of him at every turn, constantly talking to him in person or on the phone—it made it harder and harder to convince herself it was merely teenaged infatuation.

Suddenly it was so clear—being thrown together with Quentin in this quest to keep Shayna on the straight and narrow. It really was God's plan all along...His plan to get them, and keep them, together.

She wasn't sure what to make of it. Part of her was pleased. She liked thinking Quentin was part of God's plan for her. But she still had issues with him that she wasn't sure she could deal with or even work out, even though she'd promised him earlier that she'd forgive him as long as he was honest. She'd prayed about it and was determined to try.

Before she could consider it further, Shayna came back through the door.

"I forgot something." She held up a CD in one hand and a player in the other. After setting the player on the porch next to the door, she arranged the cord so it was plugged into the wall just inside the house. Then she popped the CD into the player. "Lonestar," she said before she disappeared with a quick wave and a chirpy, "Good-bye."

Amy raised a questioning eyebrow at Quentin.

"She asked me what kind of music you liked."

"My tastes aren't the same as they used to be."

"I thought you still liked Lonestar."

"Oh, I still do. But I've grown and changed. I mostly listen to Christian Contemporary. Praise music. My absolute favorites are Chris Tomlin and Josh Wilson."

"I'll have to check them out."

Amy looked at him, askance.

"You mean you've *never* listened to them?"

Quentin looked sheepish.

"I listen to the 'oldies' station. I'm listening to the same radio station we did when we were teenagers."

"It hasn't changed in all these years?"

"Actually, it did for a while. When I first came back from the navy, they were playing disco."

Amy winced.

"Then they switched to that loud stuff Shayna likes."

She made a face and Quentin laughed. It was so nice to see him laugh. She loved the way his eyes crinkled, loved the curve of his mouth, and loved...him.

It wasn't just a teenaged infatuation she'd never gotten over. She loved him.

Amy had no choice but to keep quiet while she ate her dinner. The thoughts swirled fast and furious through her mind, and silence was the only way she could keep up with them. Quentin, bless his heart, didn't try to make conversation. It was almost as if he knew she needed to be alone with her thoughts.

But as soon as she put the napkin in her plate, he

took her by surprise.

"Dance with me, Amy?" He stood and held his hand out to her. A song about honesty was just beginning to play. Amy recognized the first few words in the song and really didn't feel comfortable even listening to it, considering what tonight was really all about.

"Quentin, I—"

"Shh. Just give me this one dance before I say what I have to say. Give me this one thing, OK?"

He still expected her to not forgive him. She'd show him. The Lord was working in her heart. No matter what he said, she'd forgive him. Resting her head against his chest, she allowed herself to be swept away.

It felt so heavenly in his arms; memories of the past paled by comparison. She didn't want the song to end. She was afraid. Whatever Quentin had to confess was big enough for him to worry she'd think it unforgivable. And though she'd promised him she could forgive anything as long as he was honest, could she really?

"Mmm, this is nice." Quentin's whisper was a deep rumble in her ear and tickled her senses.

"It is," she agreed. On the CD player, the last strains of the song faded away.

"I hate to end it, but we need to get some things out of the way. Then, if you're willing, we can continue."

She nodded, not able to vocally confirm she'd be willing when she was terrified of what he would say and how she might react.

"Amy, this is hard for me."

"Me, too," she whispered. "But I need you to tell

me. *You* need you to tell me." Absently, she tugged at her pearl necklace. Its smoothness soothed her.

Quentin's gaze followed her movements and his eyes widened in surprise. "I didn't know you still had that."

Embarrassed, Amy tucked it back inside her dress. It bothered her that Quentin knew she still wore it. It laid her heart bare, so to speak.

"You know, I had every intention of meeting you that night. But something changed."

"You stopped loving me." She knew it. She'd known it all along. Hot moisture burned at the backs of her eyes. She couldn't bear to hear him confirm it. *Please, God, don't let me cry. Not now, in front of him.*

"No. Amy, no. I never stopped loving you."

"Really?" She didn't mean to sound so sarcastic, but she just didn't believe him.

"Really." Quentin's tone was firm, certain.

"What about all those years with Karen?" How could he be with Karen if he never stopped loving her?

"Much as you don't want to know this, I did love Karen."

Amy looked away. He was right. She didn't want to know this, didn't want to hear it.

"But I loved you, too. I've never stopped. I still—" He reached for her hand. He covered it with his and traced her chin with the knuckles of his other hand.

She closed her eyes briefly, letting the feelings momentarily sweep her away. When she opened her eyes, his gaze swept from her eyes to her lips and back again.

"Quentin, I—"

"Shh, don't say it if you don't mean it."

"But I do." Her voice sounded breathy in her ears.

"Wait until I say what we both know I have to. See what you feel then."

She looked away.

"OK?"

She nodded once, not daring to look at him for fear of getting lost in her emotions at a time when she must be strong. She could give in to nothing until she had the answers she sought. Again she reached for the necklace.

"I remember when I gave that to you. I can't believe you still have it after all these years." *Especially after what I did to you.* The words hung unspoken in the air.

"For keeps. That's what you said, Quentin. Did you ever mean it? If you did and you meant it just now when you said you never stopped loving me, then why? Tell me why you never showed up? Why did you dump me?" Amy couldn't control the emotion in her voice. It didn't matter anymore. Letting Quentin know she still cared, that her life had been stagnant while his had grown and changed...she couldn't be any more humiliated.

"It's a long and complicated story. But I was scared."

"What?"

"Scared. I was seventeen years old. I didn't know how I would take care of you."

"That was it?" Amy couldn't believe her ears. Was this some kind of joke?

"No." Quentin rubbed his hand across his face. "There's more. Much more."

"We had it all planned out, remember?"

"I know we did. What we didn't have was a high school diploma, money in the bank, a job lined up.

And we didn't have God's blessing."

That last bit had her instant attention. She knew right then and there where Quentin's hesitation had come from.

Oh, Lord, she prayed silently. *Why? How could You lead him from me when we were so clearly meant for each other? Was Karen really so much better a Christian than I?*

She fought to keep the tears at bay, not wanting Quentin to know how devastating this all was. To know, to have it revealed to her that God found her lacking...it was simply horrible.

It's not about someone else being better.

"Yes, it is."

"What?" Quentin looked at her when she mumbled the words under her breath.

"Nothing."

It's about timing. My timing.

Amy tried to ignore the words whispering through her heart, though a kernel of truth niggled deep inside.

"So, what? You talked to God and He told you not to meet me that night?"

"No. I mean I prayed about it, but I did something else. I went and talked to Karen."

Still fighting tears, Amy gave him a hard look.

"I loved you, Amy. But when I went to talk to Karen that night, she told me—"

"There's always a *but*, isn't there? Why can't you just say it? You loved Karen more."

"No, Amy. Karen and I were just friends at the time. I loved her as a friend. Nothing more."

"Then why did you marry her? Why would you marry someone you didn't love when you could have married someone you did?"

"It wasn't about love, Amy. That's what I'm trying to tell you." Quentin's tone was frustrated, bordering on angry. "We were too young. I was too young. I couldn't take care of you. Worrying about how I'd take care of you was keeping me awake nights, making me sick. And I didn't feel right with God. I prayed about it and felt even less right. Then I went to talk to Karen, she told me something that changed everything. That's when I made the decision that we, I, couldn't run off."

"And you couldn't even *tell* me? You just left me sitting in a bus station in the middle of the night, waiting, wondering? How did that make you right with God?"

Lips pressed together, eyes etched with pain, Quentin shook his head. "It didn't make me right with God, Amy."

Amy closed her eyes against the pain in his voice, as if that would make it all go away. But of course, it didn't. When she opened them again she found him staring at her, his eyes filled with so much emotion.

"There's more, isn't there?" She hated the flatness of her voice.

"I loved you so much," Quentin whispered. "There was no way I could look you in the eyes and tell you what I had to tell you."

"So you took the easy way out."

Quentin nodded and looked away. "I knew you'd be hurt by my decision. I couldn't face your pain. I couldn't tell you what Karen told me. So I chickened out."

Amy grabbed the necklace at her throat and held it up to him with an angry jerk.

"You said for keeps. *For keeps.* Didn't that mean anything to you?"

"Yes, Amy, but there was more going on, and I need to tell you about it."

"I don't want to hear anymore. I'd packed my things, prepared myself never to see my family again. So your being *scared* just doesn't cut it. I was scared, too. In fact, from the moment we made the decision to run away together, I was scared. But I followed through on my end. Why couldn't you?" Angry, Amy tugged hard at the necklace and was horrified when the chain broke and pooled against her hand.

"Amy, here, let me—"

"No!" She thrust the broken necklace in his hand. It was the perfect symbol of her broken dreams, not to mention her heart. "You take it. I'm leaving."

Quentin stared down at the necklace in his hands, the look on his face pure anguish. "Amy, there still more I need to tell you."

"I *don't* want to hear it." Amy tried to force that look out of her heart as she grabbed her purse and headed for her car. No matter how sorry he was, Quentin Macmillan wouldn't get the chance to break her heart again.

❧

Long after Amy left, Quentin held onto the broken necklace. It was still warm from being around her neck. Holding it in his hand now was almost like a way to be close to her. Was that how she'd felt? Wearing it all this time? That she'd even kept it touched him deep inside.

He stared out into the yard at nothing in particular. The CD player had long ago clicked off. Amy didn't understand why he'd done what he had, and he didn't blame her. He never should have said anything about being scared. He should have told her about Karen first, and maybe she would have understood. Maybe then she would have forgiven him.

For a while, he'd dared to hope she would. Especially after she'd promised to forgive him no matter what as long as he was honest with her. There was even a moment there, when it seemed she'd been about to say she loved him.

Now he wished he hadn't stopped her. Maybe then it wouldn't have been so easy for her to walk away from him.

Heavy hearted, he tucked the necklace into his jeans pocket and began to clear the table.

"Hi ya, Mr. Mac." Mrs. Parsons' gray head bobbled up on her side of the fence. Her red cheeks rounded with her smile.

Quentin restrained rolling his eyes. Even in the depths of his own pain, he'd never intentionally hurt her feelings. "Mrs. P., how are you?" He walked over toward the fence, even though he really wanted to retreat inside his house.

"I see you had some company tonight."

Amy. Just thinking about her right now hurt. "That was Amy Welsh. Shayna's journalism teacher." Quentin knew good and well, Mrs. P. knew exactly who Amy was even though she'd never admit it.

"Oh..." A sideways half-smile rounded one side of Mrs. P.'s face. "Mr. Mac, you didn't tell me you had a lady friend."

"She's just a friend." He really didn't want to tell Mrs. P. much more about Amy. He didn't want to talk about her at all.

"Well, then." Mrs. P. looked a little too pleased,

obviously not believing him. "I hope you'll introduce us the next time she's over."

Quentin was sure that would never happen. He'd be lucky if Amy ever spoke to him again, let alone grace him with her presence in his house.

"Oh, before I go." Mrs. Parson's tone sounded a little strained. "I see you've gotten rid of that duck. Good."

Something almost undetectable changed in the woman's expression—like the sparkle went out of her eyes. Quentin had the distinct feeling she wasn't telling the truth. If he had to place a bet, he'd say Mrs. P. missed Rufus. Of course, she'd never admit it.

Quentin scooped up a few of the dishes from the picnic table and nodded at his neighbor.

"Good night, Mrs. P." Not wanting to give the appearance of rudely dismissing her, he added, "I'll talk to you later. Give Foster my regards."

He swore her face lit up at the mention of her cat and knew he'd done the right thing. He'd made his lonely neighbor feel good.

Now if only someone could do the same for him.

⌒∽⌒

It was one of the hardest things she'd ever done, but Amy went to church on Sunday morning. She had to. Even though she was confused and upset by Quentin's revelation that ultimately the Lord had led him from her, she needed the comfort she'd find in an hour spent in worship service.

In the parking lot before getting out of the car, she said a short prayer for courage and strength. She was afraid to see Quentin, afraid for him to see the dark smudges under her eyes.

"I'm not strong enough to forgive him on my own, Lord. And I promised Quentin that whatever his reasons, I'd forgive him. Please help me keep that promise."

But even if she made it to the point where she could forgive him, Amy was fairly certain she wouldn't be able to forget.

No sooner did she walk through the church doors than she found herself wishing she'd stayed home. Shayna stood smack in the middle of the foyer, a huge smile on her face, obviously oblivious to last night's disaster.

"Amy— I mean Miss Welsh. How'd Rufus do last night?"

"Great, Shayna." Looking into eyes so like Quentin's, Amy forced herself to smile. "He seemed quite content this morning. He was sitting on one of the back steps when I left a little while ago."

Shayna looked so relieved, Amy wanted to hug her. But of course, she couldn't. For now, she had to keep her distance. Her heart could only take so much.

"Ashley and I want to come by and see him later. Is that OK?"

"Of course. He's yours. You can come anytime you like." *Just leave your father home.*

As if she read Amy's thoughts, she said, "Dad won't be coming. He's meeting Bradley after church."

Quentin was still meeting with Bradley? Even after last night, when he obviously thought any chance for them was gone? Surprised, and pleased, Amy realized Quentin meant what he said about forgiveness and second chances. She was the one who had some serious work to do in that area.

"Come sit with us, Miss Welsh." Shayna tugged on her sleeve.

Over Shayna's shoulder, Amy could see Quentin looking at her expectantly. Or was he looking hopeful? She was too tired to tell. He looked as though his night had been as sleepless as hers. Served him right.

Almost as if to point out the inappropriateness of such thoughts in church, the congregation began to sing.

"Not today, Shayna. I'm sitting right there." Amy indicated a pew near the back and quickly slid between two elderly ladies. "Excuse me," she whispered as she sat down. Guilt over her rudeness to Shayna plagued her. It wasn't Shayna's fault Amy and Quentin had serious issues to work out before they could be friends again.

The sermon was about grudges and forgiveness. Amy squirmed in her seat.

Quentin looked over his shoulder and their eyes met. She turned away, but the look in his eyes burned into her mind. When they sang, she could hear his voice. When they bowed their heads in prayer, she kept replaying last night's conversation. The fact that Quentin stood her up that night, just because he was scared—well it hurt worse than if it had been for any one of the reasons she'd imagined. Amy didn't know if she could ever forget how fresh and raw that pain had been.

After church she drove to a fast food drive-thru, then down to the beach to eat her lunch.

For some reason, she wasn't surprised when Quentin pulled up next to her on the passenger side. When he got out of his truck she turned to look out her window, ignoring him. He knocked on the passenger window, persistent, until she finally reached over and unlocked the door.

Hesitantly, he stuck his head in the door.

"What?" She couldn't help sounding grouchy.

"So this is what it's like inside a pink car."

"Mauve. What do you want?" *Ouch.* Amy winced right along with Quentin at her clipped, hateful tone.

"Amy, I'm sorry. Really, I am. I wish there was something, anything I could do to change the way I treated you. I've wished it every night for seventeen years. But I can't."

"You're right, you can't. You can go now."

"Amy, don't be like this." His voice was soothing, pleading.

"Why not? I'm not allowed to be hurt? I'm just supposed to let it go? Forgive you just like that? Pretend it never happened? I'm not that good a Christian, Quentin."

"I don't think it's a matter of being a 'good' Christian. I think being mad feels good and it's easier for you to hang onto these feelings than to live with the rejection and your true feelings."

"You're right. I want to stay mad and sulk. So leave."

"Amy, please? I still have more to tell you."

What more could there possibly be? She squeezed her eyes shut, trying to ignore the pull he had on her. "No. Leave."

Quentin sighed, obviously exasperated. At least he realized it was useless to argue with her. He got out of the car and stood next to his truck, the pleading look still in his eyes.

As she started the car and put it in reverse, a seagull flew overhead—the inspiration for a very wicked thought.

Amy pushed the button and rolled down the passenger window.

"Quentin, there's one more thing."

A hopeful look lit his eyes and he stepped toward her. At the same moment, Amy tossed her uneaten hamburger across the car seat and out the open window. It landed at Quentin's feet but stayed there only a fraction of a second before it was besieged upon by a flurry of wings. Somewhere amidst the screaming seagulls, stood Quentin and it gave her a feeling of satisfaction to know he wouldn't be able to escape without at least a little bit of seagull mess landing on him and his shining black truck.

14

"I'm sorry, Lord. Why can't I just let go and be nice? I don't understand what's happening to me."

Horrified to realize what she'd just done to Quentin, Amy pulled over to the side of the road. Should she go back and apologize? She'd been totally irrational. All that talk about forgiving Quentin as long as he was honest...well, it went right out of her heart as soon as he told her why he'd stood her up.

Turning her car toward home, Amy realized Quentin would be in no mood to talk to her after the seagulls finished with him. Once there, she walked aimlessly around the house with a dust rag, waiting for a decent amount of time to pass before she could call Quentin. When she finally did call, there was no answer. Ashamed, she realized he probably needed to shower, change, and wash his truck.

After she washed the dishes, she tried again. Still no answer. He probably had caller ID and didn't want to talk to her. Not that she blamed him. She wouldn't want to talk to herself, either. Her behavior was inexcusable.

After peeling a few leaves from a head of lettuce, Amy went out to the backyard. She tried to coax Rufus over, but he wouldn't come near her. He probably had some weird duck sense and knew what she'd done to his master.

Amy sat down on the steps to the back porch and

tore the lettuce into tiny pieces. Then she tossed a little to Rufus.

"If you're really patient, you can get him to take it out of your hand."

Startled, Amy looked up to see Quentin standing near the gate. Still damp from a shower, his hair was neatly combed even though one dark wave fell across his forehead.

His expression was one of uncertainty, lacking any sort of smile.

Surprised, relieved, Amy just stared. Never before had the sight of Quentin been so good. She'd been so sure he'd never want to see her again, that she'd never have a chance to apologize. She could feel the blush, the shame, washing over her.

"Quentin, I'm really sorry."

"How sorry?"

Confused, she watched him walk toward her. The dark blue shirt fit him just right, making him appear huggable, and brought out the richness of his eyes.

"What do you mean?"

"Are you sorry enough to go somewhere with me after youth group tonight, so we can talk about it?"

Talk? She wasn't ready to talk. Was she? She wanted to, but...she didn't want to, but...she needed to.

"Where?"

"I don't care. Anywhere. We need to clear this up."

Whether or not it was possible to ever settle things between them, Amy had to try.

Finally, she nodded. "OK."

"Great." The uncertainty faded from Quentin's face and a smile lifted the corners of his mouth. Amy had a hard time not smiling back.

"You clean up pretty nice." The words were out of her mouth before she realized it. Amy couldn't believe she'd been so bold.

"Thanks. Now give me that lettuce and let me show you how it's done."

Their fingertips touched when she handed him the lettuce. She wanted more, wanted him to take advantage of the moment and cover her hand with his. But he didn't. Instead, he demonstrated with great patience, how to coax the duck over to eat out of his hand.

When Amy tried it, the duck only came so far. He'd get within two feet of her and stop. Then he'd back way off and they'd start the whole process again.

"I give up." Dejected, Amy plopped herself back on the porch. "He's never going to warm to me."

"It just takes time, Amy. You have to be patient."

"No." She shook her head. "That isn't it at all. He *knows*."

"Knows what? He's a duck." Quentin looked at her like she was crazy.

"He knows what I did to you. He's snubbing me."

Quentin laughed. "Just keep on trying. I've got to go now. I have a few things to do at the office before Bradley shows up for our meeting."

"Oh, yeah." Amy had almost forgotten. "Good luck." She smiled to show she meant it, and he dropped a kiss on her cheek.

"Listen, Amy." Quentin's tone was serious, as was the look in his eyes. "More than anything, I want your forgiveness. If it never goes beyond that, then OK. But it is as important to be forgiven as it is to forgive. Just remember that, OK?"

Not trusting herself to speak, she simply nodded.

"See you tonight," he whispered.

Hope lifted Amy's spirit and battled with the uncertainty still there. Quentin had forgiven her act of meanness. Was it, then, possible for her to forgive him for doing something he thought was right?

It was, but only with the help of the Lord.

She thought about it a minute and realized she wasn't as upset as she was earlier.

෬෨

Finally Quentin had something to feel positive about. He'd finagled more than one smile out of Amy and come away with the promise they could talk again. Tonight. His relief was immeasurable.

He headed his truck toward his office building, anxious to put this meeting with Bradley behind him. Hopefully they'd come away with a new understanding.

Russ's truck sat in the parking lot in front of the building. Strange. Russ didn't usually go to the office on Sunday. He must have left something behind.

The timing wasn't the best since Bradley was on his way, but maybe they'd have at least a few minutes in private with no distractions. Quentin really wanted to find out what was bothering Russ, and he felt bad that he hadn't pressed the issue sooner.

Quentin let himself in the front door, ready for some guy talk. But just before he called out a greeting, he stopped short. Something wasn't right. Russ stood just inside Quentin's office, talking on the phone. It was odd because Russ had a phone at his own desk. He had no reason to be in Quentin's office.

After taking a step forward, Quentin stopped

again. The conversation taking place...a sick feeling curled through his insides.

"That's right. Macmillan's bid is three-quarters of a mil for the first set of condos, and half a mil for each of the others. You should have no problem coming in well under that with the cut-rate you get on materials."

This couldn't be right. Russ giving away inside information to a competing company? Not very likely. There must be some sort of mistake. It couldn't be what it appeared.

Quentin stepped closer and noticed the plans for the condo project spread out across his desk. Plans he deliberately hadn't shown anyone. The condo project was supposed to help get his business back on track. Back on track after being out-bid on one project after another.

Russ was listening to whoever was on the other end of the phone, rubbing the back of his neck as if he had a tension headache. "Yeah, right. You'll come out of it with a nice little profit. When can I expect payment?"

Not giving information away, selling it. Quentin's blood ran cold.

"That's not soon enough. I need—but my wife—"

Quentin watched Russ grow more and more agitated before he muttered something and hung up the phone. When he turned around and saw Quentin standing there, he jumped and his face flushed.

"Quentin, I'm sorry, I—"

"Don't even bother." Quentin wanted to pulverize him. He stepped toward him, fists clenched, one arm raised. Fear flickered in Russ's eyes, and Quentin restrained himself. Not an easy task. "I don't want to hear your sorry explanation," he said through clenched teeth.

"You don't under—"

"You're right I don't. You've just taken my daughter's future and flushed it down the toilet. Because of you I'll have to lay off some of the guys. And I'll probably have to dip into Shayna's college fund just to get by. There's not much you can say that'll make any of it right."

Shame-faced, Russ looked down at his shoes. "I know," he muttered.

Quentin wanted to punch something. Preferably Russ's face. But he wasn't a violent man. He settled for upending the desk. Russ flinched as it crashed to the floor and paper and drafting tools scattered everywhere. For the moment, Quentin didn't care.

"I thought I was failing my daughter. Called myself every sort of loser. You even listened to me worry about it. What kind of friend are you? Get your things and get out."

Russ didn't protest. He walked out of Quentin's office and headed toward the door. Quentin watched his friend walk out without so much as a backward glance. Russ didn't even walk over to his own desk and retrieve the "World's Best Dad" coffee mug his son had given him for his birthday last year. Something about Russ wasn't quite right, and it went far beyond selling out his boss, co-workers, and friends.

After Russ drove away, Quentin cleaned up the mess he'd made, all the while wondering how his friend could betray him. And why? He just didn't understand. It was so out of character for Russ. Something was terribly wrong, and he intended to find out. He searched for a piece of notepaper, and hastily scribbled a message to Bradley. They could meet later.

Right now he had to catch up with Russ.

He tacked the note to the outside door. Hopefully Bradley would understand. Then he sprinted toward his truck and jumped in the cab. He was around the first sharp curve in the road when he realized he hadn't fastened his seatbelt. He reached down to fumble with it, and at the same moment a rabbit darted in front of him. Out of instinct he swerved and slammed on the brakes at the same time. He struggled for control of the swaying truck, but was powerless to stop it as it slid head-on toward a massive oak.

∂∽∾

Amy put the dust rag away and washed her hands. At this rate, she'd have the cleanest house in town. But dusting gave her a diversion. Something to take her mind off the fact that Quentin was almost two hours late. She couldn't help wondering if he'd stood her up again.

This time, she wasn't just disappointed for herself. She'd been anxious to hear how the talk with Bradley went. If Quentin had decided to give Bradley a chance, it meant *Amy* could give *Quentin* a chance. The thought was always at the back of her mind, alternately teasing and torturing her.

Perhaps things hadn't gone well with Bradley, and Quentin didn't want to tell her about it. Or it was possible the youth group ran late. But certainly not this late. Two hours? Something could have happened to one of the kids, but surely Quentin would have called.

No, her first assumption had to be right. Quentin didn't want to face up to a tough conversation.

Amy had just been stood up...again.

It was obvious he had feelings for her and wanted to rekindle something. And she was more than a little interested. But there were some lines she wouldn't cross.

Being stood up more than once was the biggest. Playing second fiddle to Karen's memory was another. It was too easy to get caught up in wondering if Quentin wanted her just because Karen wasn't there and he needed to fill up the empty space. She didn't want to be a substitute for Karen. She wanted to be cherished and loved for herself, obviously something she'd never be as far as Quentin was concerned. If it was, he wouldn't have risked hurting her again.

Quentin had just proved once more he couldn't be trusted.

જીન્જી

The school day was nearly at an end. Amy had one class to go. She'd checked her cell phone several times, and she'd also been to the office several times that day to check her messages hoping there was some remote chance Quentin had called her with a simple explanation for blowing her off last night. Thus far there'd been no messages, and she'd been a major source of irritation to the school secretary.

After this last class was over, Amy planned to go home and soak in a nice hot tub with a good book. Then she'd go to bed early. And tonight she wouldn't waste on minute's sleep on Quentin Macmillan. It had been a long day, preceded by an even longer night. Amy's eyes were heavy. They felt like sandpaper. She'd lain awake most of last night.

As the students filed in, she found herself

searching for Shayna. There was no sign of her. Bradley sat in the back of the room, alone, and fifteen minutes after class began Amy stopped expecting her to walk through the door.

She thought about calling Quentin to make sure Shayna was all right but figured it would look like a vain attempt to see why he stood her up last night. She wasn't about to stoop to that level.

Quentin Macmillan had no place in her thoughts or her heart, and it was high time she accepted it.

After class was over, she erased the blackboard then gathered her things. She was about to flip off the lights when Bradley came back in the door.

"Excuse me, Miss Welsh. Do you have a minute?"

"Sure, Bradley. Did you forget something?"

"Yeah. It's Mr. Macmillan. Shayna wanted me to tell you about last night. I wasn't sure if you'd heard, and I didn't want to tell you in front of everyone—just in case."

"What are you talking about?" Alarmed, Amy clutched her briefcase tight to her chest.

"There—he—"

"Bradley?" Her tone was sharper than she intended. "What is it?"

"He's in the hospital. There was an accident yesterday afternoon. Quentin wrecked his truck."

Amy didn't wait for the rest. She raced down the hall, still clutching her briefcase. It didn't matter that there was a rule about running in the halls. She had to get to Quentin.

࿐

Amy stood in the doorway, breath held, watching

Quentin as he slept in the uncomfortable looking hospital bed. At first glance, he appeared far too healthy to be here. Thank the Lord. His color was good, and he didn't even have an IV.

So many feelings flooded her. She wanted to step inside the room but was afraid. What would his reaction be? Would he be happy to see her, or would he wonder why she wasn't here last night? She really had no right to be here. Especially since she, once again, had leapt to the wrong conclusion and been conceited enough to think it was all about her. Why hadn't she stopped to think something might be wrong?

She really owed him an apology.

As quiet as possible, she tiptoed over to the bed. Now that she was closer she could see the bruises on his forehead and right side of his face. She started to reach out and caress his cheek but pulled her hand back at the last instant.

Quentin stirred and his eyelids fluttered. Squinting as if trying to bring her face into focus, he finally smiled.

"Amy?"

"Hey," she said softly. "How are you doing?"

"Better now that you're here." He reached for her, and she willingly took his hand. It was firm and warm, and he curled it around hers.

"I would have been here sooner but I— I didn't know. Bradley just told me a few minutes ago."

"Bradley." Quentin caressed the back of her hand with his thumb. "He's a good kid."

Amy couldn't help but smile. "I told you."

"Did he tell you he's the one who found me? He called 9-1-1 and stayed with me until they arrived.

Then he called Shayna."

"He's not as bad as you thought, is he?"

"Not at all. He acted very responsibly."

"I'm glad. Can I get you anything?"

"Nothing." He patted the bed, somewhere in the vicinity of his knees. "Just sit."

"Are you sure I should?"

"*I* think you should, so I'm sure it's OK." He spoke in a sleepy, lazy manner. "They want their patients to be happy."

Amy felt her heart catch. Quentin was hurting, yet he intimated that having her nearby would make him happy. Smoothing the spot he'd indicated, she sat.

"So, tell me what happened. How did you wreck your truck?"

"Sheer stupidity. I was so distracted; I had no business on the road. None."

He told her about Russ Miller, and his betrayal of their friendship. "I still can't believe he did this."

"What are you going to do?"

Quentin shrugged. "I'm not going to have him arrested or anything like that. But I can't afford to have him working for me, either."

"I'm sure he'd be too embarrassed to come back, anyway."

"Probably. I know Russ, and the humiliation will eat at him until it destroys him. That, in itself, is bad enough."

Quentin's eyes drifted shut as his voice grew softer. Amy recognized exhaustion when she saw it.

"Let's not talk about it anymore right now. You need to rest." She started to rise, but he held tight to her hand. Perhaps he wasn't as exhausted as she thought.

"Amy," he whispered thickly. "Don't leave me."

The plea tore at her heart. Was he asking her to stay at the hospital or stay in his life? She suspected a little of both, and she wanted him to mean both. But was she ready to step past the humiliation and pain he'd caused her?

It was certainly well past time. But it was easier said than done.

As if he sensed her inner struggle, Quentin opened his eyes. He tried to sit up, but Amy managed to convince him to stay put.

"Is there something else you need?"

Relaxing back against the pillows, Quentin whispered one more thing before he let go of her hand. "Forgiveness, Amy. Remember?"

"I remember, Quentin. And I'm trying." As soon as she spoke the words, she knew she truly meant them.

"Good. Thank you. I hope you'll still feel that way when I tell you the rest."

The rest. A chill shimmied up Amy's spine. Quentin watched her with an odd expression and she couldn't help but wonder what he was thinking.

"Is something wrong? Do you need something?"

Quentin continued to watch her for a moment before nodding. "Ice chips."

The paper cup of ice chips sat on his bedside tray. Amy shook off her sense of foreboding, stood from the bed and picked up the ice chips. As she did, Quentin tried to reach for them. "No." She shook her head. "Let me do it."

He made a face, but she lifted the spoon of ice to his lips. It was the least she could do. When she set the cup down, he reached for her hand.

"Amy, don't be mad at me, OK?"

"Why on earth would I be mad?"

"Because I didn't show up last night."

"Of course, I'm not mad. I'm just glad you're going to be OK."

He was strangely quiet.

"Quentin? You *are* going to be OK, aren't you?"

"That's the other reason you might be mad."

Confused, she stared at him. He reached out and stroked her cheek, then gestured for her to move away. She stepped back, still confused even when Quentin sat up without a struggle.

"I'm going to be just fine. The doctor left just before you got here and said I could go home as soon as someone could pick me up. I heard you talking to the nurse in the hallway, so I pretended to be asleep." He looked sheepish. "I guess I wanted you to give me some tender loving care."

She wasn't mad. She wanted to smack him with his pillow, but she wasn't mad. In fact...she was kind of pleased.

"Amy, my truck's a wreck. Would you take me home?"

In that moment her heart felt lighter and she knew the Lord had just lifted a little more of the pain from her heart.

15

It wasn't quite daylight when Amy stepped out on the back porch on Thursday morning. She had to get an early start this morning. It seemed the closer it grew to the end of the school year, the more work there was to do and the only way to finish everything was to go in early.

She walked down to the pen to let Rufus out, and thought of Quentin. She couldn't help it. Every time she looked at his duck, she thought about him. He was doing well, the soreness had eased, and he was planning to go back to work today. His truck was being repaired, and he had to drive a rental car that he kept complaining about.

She hadn't seen him since Monday night when she'd taken him home from the hospital, though they'd talked on the phone a few times. She'd just been too busy with school. At least that's what she'd managed to convince herself.

Truthfully, Amy was more than a little afraid of her feelings for him. They'd grown. Changed. They weren't the same feelings she'd had as a teenager. They weren't even the same feelings she'd experienced after they'd spent the evening together at the drive-in. This was something much greater.

If she had to pinpoint what had changed, she'd have to say it began with the forgiveness. Once Amy realized she wasn't upset with him any longer, something in her heart changed. She no longer looked at Quentin with suspicion, like he was going to hurt her again. She still felt like she was second-rate to Karen and really didn't understand why it was OK for Quentin to marry Karen so soon after Amy left town. But she was dealing with it.

After putting food out for the duck, she headed back into the house to do a final check of the kitchen before leaving for work. The iron was unplugged; the stove was off. Amy gathered her briefcase and purse from the kitchen table then glanced out the window. Perhaps she should grab a sweater. It was gray, overcast, and didn't look like the sun had any intention of coming out today.

A flurry of movement in the yard caught her eye and she stepped closer to the window.

At first she thought it was a cat, but it was too big. She opened the back door. At the sound, the animal raised its head. A raccoon. A cute, furry little bandit. He stared straight at her for a fraction of a second, then bent his head and went back to whatever he was doing.

It took another split second for Amy to realize what the raccoon had in its grasp. When she did, she gasped and raced down the steps.

"Get away! Go," she screamed. The raccoon looked at her but didn't move.

"Go!" Amy screamed again and ran closer.

Frantically, she looked around for something to throw. Nothing. She pulled off her shoe and threw it at the animal. The raccoon fled.

"Rufus. Oh, Rufus." Amy ran over to the injured duck. He lay on the ground near his pen. His neck was bent at a funny angle and blood dampened his green feathers.

She raced to the house and grabbed a towel and her cell phone. After she had the duck wrapped as best she could, she punched in Quentin's number.

"Quentin! A raccoon. The duck. He's bad. I don't know what to do. Please hurry!"

"I'll be right there."

Five minutes later, Quentin pulled up in his little rental car, unshaven, hair rumpled, in gray sweats, smelling of minty toothpaste.

Amy was never so glad to see anyone in her life.

"Here, let me see him." She scooted out of the way while Quentin bent over to unwrap the towel. He sucked in a breath and his face tightened in concern.

"He's not dead, but he is suffering." Quentin gently pulled the towel back around Rufus then scooped him into his arms.

"Quentin, I'm so sorry. It's morning. I never thought..."

"Shh." He planted a kiss on her forehead, and then stood. "It's not your fault. Come on. You drive."

"Where?"

"To Nick St. James. He'll know what to do. If we can save Rufus without him suffering too much, he'll know. If we need to—" He broke off, silent for a moment, lips pressed together. "He'll know that, too."

After she shut the car door, Amy cradled her head against the steering wheel. She felt sick.

"Are you OK?"

Fighting tears, she nodded but didn't look up. The concern in Quentin's voice touched her. Her guilt-feeling was overwhelming. The poor duck. He was suffering, might even die, because of her stupidity.

"If you want to hold Rufus, I'll drive."

"No." She lifted her head then, and looked at Quentin through tear-filled eyes.

"I'm so sorry, Quentin. I should have known it wasn't light enough outside. I feel so stupid."

"It's really not your fault." He reached over and brushed a stray curl off her forehead and gave her a sad little half-crooked smile. "Don't blame yourself."

Amy put the car in gear and backed out of the driveway. She drove to Nick's, her heart thumping hard with fear and desperation. They had to get there in time.

On the seat next to her, Quentin sat stroking the top of Rufus's head and whispering in a soothing voice. Every once in a while Rufus made a sad little croaking sound. It was enough to break Amy's heart.

"Did you tell Shayna?"

"No." Quentin sighed, leaned his head back and closed his eyes. "I thought it best to wait until we know if we can save the little guy."

Amy nodded, understanding completely.

Please, Father, don't let us have to give Shayna bad news. Please help Nick do what he must to help Rufus.

"Turn here."

Nick's property was huge. Any other time, Amy would have taken a moment to revel in the view, but today she was more concerned about the duck.

She barely had the car at a standstill when Quentin was out the door and up the steps. He banged on Nick's door without any attempt at politeness.

Nick opened the door and immediately took the duck.

Amy followed behind him and Quentin, to the kitchen.

"It's not as bad as it looks." Nick said after careful

examination. "I think he'll be fine in no time."

Amy let out a pent-up breath and gave Quentin a weak smile. He took her hand and squeezed it gently.

"I'll have to do some sewing, though." Nick turned to Quentin. "I need you to hold him still. Amy, you might want to sit in the living room."

"No, I'll wait here."

"OK." He didn't argue, but sounded skeptical like he expected her to run for the door any second. He rummaged through a drawer. "Let me just sterilize this needle."

"I— I think I'd better go call the school. I left my phone in the car."

"You can use mine." Nick nodded toward the phone on the wall next to his kitchen counter.

"No, I'll just go outside and use my own. The number is already pre-programmed."

A knowing look passed between Quentin and Nick. Amy knew she sounded like an idiot. She knew they knew she was making an excuse, but she didn't care. She just had to get out of there.

Half an hour later, Quentin walked out to the car to get her. He pulled her door open, and looked down at her with concern in his eyes.

"You can come back in now."

Amy nodded and swallowed hard. "How is he?"

"He'll be fine. He's sore, of course, but Nick gave me a topical antiseptic that also helps numb the area. We just have to apply it every couple of hours. It's a flesh wound. The skin was torn back, but no arteries were severed."

She closed her eyes against the image she'd conjured up. "I just feel so bad."

"I know you do. But really, it's not your fault.

Don't beat yourself up over it."

Amy nodded, but she really didn't mean it.

As if sensing the truth, Quentin reached out to help Amy from the car. "How about you and I take the day off? We can take care of Rufus together and just try and feel better. What do you think?"

It sounded nice. She'd have to get a substitute, but since she had already called in for the morning getting the sub to stay the rest of the day shouldn't be that difficult.

They took the duck back to Amy's house, and Quentin made him a nice cozy spot in the corner of the kitchen. They watched him for a while, making sure he was as comfortable as possible.

Amy made tuna salad sandwiches and served them with chips and soda.

"One of the guys at work talked to Russ." Quentin waited for her to sit down at the table before he continued. "His wife's been gambling at the casino down in the Skagit Flats. It started out small, but escalated before he even realized it. He was trying desperately to keep them from losing everything."

"Wow."

"What he did with the bids was illegal. But I can't turn him in. I can't have him prosecuted. We've been friends for so many years. I just can't bring myself to do it."

Amy noticed he spoke of their friendship in the present-tense. He was leaps and bounds ahead of her in the forgiveness department. To think, she'd once accused him of not being able to forgive.

"Quentin, you're not planning to hire him back?"

He looked at her thoughtfully, and then nodded. "I'm going to see him when I leave here."

At her incredulous look, he added, "I have no choice. He's my friend. If I don't give him his job back, he won't be able to afford the kind of help his wife needs. I haven't mentioned it to him yet, but that's my plan."

When she didn't comment, Quentin assured her Russ would work only in a supervised capacity, with no access to confidential documents.

Amy hoped it worked. She couldn't stand for Quentin to be hurt again. Only Quentin could be so kind-hearted toward someone who so totally betrayed him. There weren't many men like him. A feeling of warmth filled her heart.

When they finished eating, Quentin broached the subject they'd both been avoiding.

"Have you decided to forgive me yet?" He watched her closely and she struggled not to squirm under his gaze.

"It's not that."

He looked at her in disbelief. "What do you mean? You've told me repeatedly it's about forgiveness."

"No, I don't mean that."

"Amy, you're confusing me. What are you talking about?"

"It's the humiliation. I've figured out how to forgive you, but I haven't figured out how to get over the humiliation."

"Amy, I can't fix what I did to you. All I can do is apologize."

She saw the truth of his words. "I know that, Quentin. I really do. And I do forgive you. I still don't quite understand, but I do forgive you."

He took her hand and held it to her lips, his steady blue gaze caressing her face.

"Thank you. You don't know how much this means to me. Amy, I—"

"Shh. Quentin, I don't want to talk about that night right now. I said I forgive you. But I can't go beyond that right now."

Quietly, he nodded. "I need to tell you—"

"I need you to tell me about Karen." Amy couldn't believe she said it, but it was too late to call back the words.

"What do you want to know?"

"Maybe if I knew why, it would help." She lifted her chin and looked him square in the eye. "If you were so afraid to run off with me, then why did you marry Karen so soon after I left? And in high school no less. What was the difference?"

His long silence told her he struggled with the answer. The fact that he wouldn't look her in the eye told her she wouldn't like the answer. Mentally she braced herself for whatever he was about to say.

"There wasn't one."

"That's it? That's your answer?" She shook her head in anger. "Don't even try it, Quentin. You and Karen had a nice happy life. You didn't live in the dumps. You can't tell me there wasn't a difference."

"Amy, I honestly don't know what to say. No matter what I say, we're going to end up right back where we were, with you not forgiving me. And that's not what I want."

She stared at the floor, contemplating the truth of his words. Finally, she looked up. "I promise whatever you say, I won't take a step back. OK? I just want to know about her. How you fell in love with her. Why? What kind of life you had together. What did she have that I didn't?"

"Amy, it wasn't like that."

"What was it like then?"

"That's what I was trying to tell you before."

That foreboding she felt in the hospital was back. She didn't want to hear whatever he was going to say. But she had to. It was the only way they could move forward. "OK, tell me then."

Reluctantly, he finally agreed. "If we'd run off to California, I wouldn't have finished school. Without that high school diploma, I wouldn't have been able to support you."

"That makes no sense, Quentin. You married Karen before you finished school."

"I know." His sigh was heavy as he broke eye contact and looked somewhere over her shoulder. Clearly there was something more he wasn't telling her.

"There's something else I don't understand. How did you go from wanting to be a photo-journalist, to joining the military?"

"I had no choice."

"What do you mean?"

"Amy, Karen was pregnant."

Amy felt sick. If Quentin had smacked her, he couldn't have startled her more.

"Pregnant? But Shayna's not—"

"Shayna's not old enough. I know. Karen lost the baby a few months after we were married."

Amy placed her hand on his shoulder. "Quentin, I'm so sorry."

He nodded. "It was pretty sad." He reached up and covered her hand with his. "It wasn't my baby, Amy."

Amy stared at him in shock. "It wasn't?"

"The baby was my brother's."

"Oh. Wow." The import of what he was saying hit her. "Your brother wouldn't marry her?"

"No. Aidan left town as soon as she told him and never looked back. She told me the night I was supposed to meet you."

"That's why you didn't show up. You married her so her baby, your niece or nephew, would have a father."

Quentin remained quiet and as he did, her admiration for him grew.

"You sacrificed your future for a child who was never born."

Still silent, Quentin stared out the window.

"Tell me something, Quentin. Why did you stay married to her after that?"

"Because I made a vow before God. For better or worse. Because to dump a woman who'd just lost her baby would be unbelievably cruel. And Amy?" Quentin turned toward her then, an odd expression on his face. "I'm not going to sit here and tell you I never loved Karen. We were always good friends and I grew to love her very much."

It only made sense. Quentin was a gentle, loving man. He'd never share a home, a life, a child with someone without giving his heart.

They were both silent for a while, lost in their thoughts. When Amy realized Quentin was watching her, she forced the images of him and Karen out of her head. It wasn't easy, but it was something she needed to work on.

"Whatever happened to your brother?"

Quentin shook his head sadly. "He could be dead for all I know. After he left town, we never heard from him again. I don't know whether or not you remember, but he was always giving my parents a bad time. Sometimes I think their worrying over Aidan is what killed both of them." There was a hint of regret in his tone.

Her tears fell unchecked, and Quentin gently rubbed them away. The lump in her throat grew, but Amy had to speak around it because the words she had to say were so very important.

"I'm proud of you."

It was true. Quentin had a big heart, and it never seemed to run out of compassion for others.

Forgiving Russ, marrying Karen and then staying with her after she lost the baby that belonged to his brother. Amy was sure that if Quentin's brother were to walk through the door right now, he'd forgive him without a second thought.

She wanted to be just like him.

おくら

Quentin knocked on the door of the Miller house, half certain no one would answer once they looked out the window and saw him standing there. His suspicion was confirmed when he saw the flutter of the living room drapes and no one opened the door.

Disappointed, a little sad, he started to step off the porch. The faint sound of the doorknob turning stopped him in his tracks. Slowly he looked back toward the door, surprised to see Janice peering out at him.

"Quentin," she said quietly. "Come in." She stepped back and pulled the door wide.

Standing in the foyer, he studied Janice. Deep,

wide half-circles smudged the skin under her eyes. She was pale, a ghost of the woman he once knew, and she avoided his gaze.

"How are you?" It was a dumb question, considering her appearance. But it was the only thing he could think of to say, and he wanted her to know that in spite of the circumstances, he cared.

She shrugged one shoulder and gave him an insincere half-smile. "Russ is in the living room," she said. "Go on in." Before he could respond, she disappeared down the hall.

The house was quiet. No TV or radio, no noisy teenagers. Quentin didn't believe he'd ever seen this house so quiet. He stepped into the living room and hesitated.

"She's mortified by her behavior." Russ sat on the couch in the dimly lit living room. He looked haggard and drawn...and worried. "You're the last person I expected to see here."

"Russ." Quentin walked over to the couch.

An awkward moment passed while the two men simply avoided each other's gaze.

"I'm mortified, too." Russ buried his face in his palms.

"I know." Quentin could lecture his friend, or listen and accept his remorse. He chose the latter.

"Janice is sick." Russ looked at Quentin, his eyes full of uncertainly. "She can't help it."

Quentin nodded and sat down in the chair opposite Russ.

"It's this adrenaline thing. I read about it somewhere, and I need to learn more about it. Some people, when they win at gambling, adrenaline is released into their system. It's addictive, that feeling, and they find themselves trying to attain that same feeling over and over. I think that's what happened to Janice."

"Is she going into therapy?"

"Yeah. Eventually. I have to find a job first. And who'll hire me after what I did to you?"

"I will."

"What I did was wrong." Russ continued talking as if he didn't hear what Quentin said. "It wasn't a sickness, like Janice. It was the worst thing I could have done to my family, and to you."

"You thought you were doing the right thing."

"No, I didn't. I knew what I was doing the entire time. It was eating me up, but I was so desperate to keep up with the money Janice was losing. I should have come to you. I know that now."

"Russ?" Quentin held something out to his friend, but Russ didn't seem to notice.

"I'll try and find some way to repay you. I promise. And I've already made a start. I told the guys at Integrity that you wouldn't prosecute them if they agreed to withdraw their bid on the bank and forget they ever heard about the condo project."

"Really?" Quentin was surprised, and more relieved than he thought possible. If he won the bid on the bank by default, financially, he'd be fine. If the condo project went through, well...he'd be more than fine and his business would be back on the right track.

"I hope you can forgive me someday, Quent."

"Done."

"What?" Russ looked at him in disbelief.

"Done. I already have. Now will you take this?"

When Russ finally saw what Quentin held, a smile spread over his face...a smile reminiscent of the old

Russ, the Russ who had been his friend for years. The Russ who would be his friend for many years to come.

"I've got a desk with an empty spot on it, just waiting for the right coffee mug to call it home."

When Russ took his "World's Best Dad" mug from him, Quentin pulled his friend into a hug. "Welcome back," he whispered. "Friend."

16

They were wrapped in each other's arms. The kiss appeared awkward and hurried. They didn't really seem to be enjoying it much but Amy knew once they made it past the shy stage, kissing could lead teenagers down a dangerous path.

"Lighthouse Point," Bradley whispered.

"Tomorrow." Shayna's hurried agreement was equally as breathless.

Lighthouse Point? Alarmed, Amy knew she had to talk to Quentin right away. In their day, Lighthouse Point was the favorite make-out spot for teenagers. And she was fairly sure things hadn't changed *that* much over the years. Secluded and woodsy, with a gorgeous view of the water, the Point was an old army base from the early 1900s that was now a state park. Between the lighthouse, the army bunkers, and the view, it was the perfect setting for romance.

Guilt weighed heavy on her shoulders. If only she'd taken Quentin's concerns more seriously and separated the kids in the beginning. But no, she'd had to stick by her principles and use what she'd learned in psychology. If something happened between Shayna and Bradley, and Shayna lost her innocence, Amy would never forgive herself.

Quentin would never forgive her, either.

Amy conjured up a mental picture of Quentin and the flame that seemed to light his eyes whenever he spoke of Shayna.

Without hesitation, she raced into her empty classroom and dialed her cell phone.

"I'm sorry. He's out of the office. May I help you instead?" Amy thought the secretary sounded a little too interested.

"Look," Amy said. She was in too much of a hurry to care that she sounded rude. "It's really important that I speak with him."

"Like I said, Miss—?"

There was a long, drawn out pause while Amy tapped her foot impatiently.

"Welsh. Amy Welsh."

"Like I said, Miss Welsh, he's out of the office. He said he wouldn't be returning for the rest of the day."

"Did he go home?"

"I can't release that information." The secretary's tone turned cool.

"Look. If he calls, have him call me. Tell him it's important. It's—" she hesitated before saying in a rush, "It's an emergency."

"What number can—?"

"He knows what it is." Amy snapped her cell phone shut then instantly regretted her rudeness. She grabbed her purse and briefcase, and headed to the office with a sense of urgency.

The school secretary looked up in alarm. "Is everything all right?"

"No. Could you let Miki Loretta know I won't be meeting her this afternoon. Tell her I had to go somewhere. Thanks."

When Amy left the school she headed for Quentin's house, but his rental car was nowhere in sight. She drove around town—the main street along the beach, then the adjacent one that ran along the business sector. No sign of him. Once more past his house without luck, then Amy turned toward home.

After racing through the door, she tried his office again. He still hadn't returned. She called his house and left a message on his voice mail, and then did the same with his cell phone.

She checked on the duck then put water in the microwave for some tea.

She tried Quentin's house again. This time the line was busy. Didn't he have call waiting?

Settling down at the table with her cup of orange spice tea, Amy asked God for the patience to wait for Shayna or Quentin to get off the phone and for the calmest way to talk to Quentin about this newest development. She also prayed for a way to get Shayna and Bradley away from each other.

Amy wasn't sure, as she sipped her tea, but it seemed the knot between her shoulders loosened just a tiny bit.

If only she could let go all the way and allow the Lord to heal her heart.

She sat up straight. Where had that thought come from?

"Please, Father, be with Shayna. Help her resist temptation. Help her realize she's much too young for a serious relationship. And Father, help me with the right words to explain to Quentin how sorry I am about all of this."

છે∽ઉ

"I'm telling you, Ashley. They spent the whole day together."

Quentin wasn't deliberately eavesdropping. He'd walked by his daughter's room, heard Amy's name, and stopped. More out of idle curiosity than parental-nosiness. Now, however, it was the nosiness that had him rooted to the spot.

"I love Rufus," she was saying, "and would never wish anything bad on him. But I tell you, it was like God put the raccoon there. Of course," she was quick to add, "God also made sure Rufus didn't get hurt really bad. Just bad enough that Amy and my dad spent the whole day together."

The tiny hairs on the back of his neck prickled. Shayna was up to something, there was no doubt.

"Yeah, it's like God is with us in this. He wants Amy and my dad together, too."

Ever so slightly, Quentin pushed against Shayna's door until the crack was wide enough for him to see through. Shayna sprawled on her bed, stomach down, feet at the head of the bed, head at the foot. Her knees were bent, and she swung her heels back and forth. Propped on her elbows, she had the phone stuck to one ear while she doodled on a pad in front of her.

"Yeah, I think it might have worked. You should have seen her. I know, gross. But it was for a good cause. Amy will be sure and tell my dad, and they'll plan another spying mission."

The words made no sense. What exactly had Shayna done? He nudged the door open the rest of the way. Folding his arms across his chest, he stood in the doorway and glowered at his daughter who was so engrossed in her conversation she'd yet to notice him.

"Mentioning Lighthouse Point—it was inspired. Your mom said they used to go there all the time. It ought to bring back some good memories. Maybe he'll kiss—"

Unmistakably loud, Quentin cleared his throat.

Shayna jerked her head up, her eyes widening with guilt.

"Uh— I gotta go!"

She swung her legs around and jumped up from the bed. Throwing the phone onto her pillow, she flashed Quentin a thousand watt smile. It wouldn't work this time.

"Daddy, uh— hi."

"Hi yourself, kiddo." He kept his arms folded and didn't smile. "What's going on?"

"On?" She stared, openmouthed, as if searching for the right excuse. "Um— Nothing. Ashley and I were just making plans."

"Yeah, I heard."

"Um...how much did you hear?"

"Enough to know you're up to something. Now spill it."

Shayna squirmed. "OK, but just remember this. I wanted you to be happy. I don't like seeing you lonely."

"Shayna." Quentin scowled and deepened his tone so his daughter knew she'd better not mess with him. "The truth, and I want it now."

Eyes wide, but showing no bit of shame, she nodded.

"It started out as a lark. When Ashley's mom told us about you and Miss Welsh, I just wanted to see if the spark was still there. And when I first mentioned her name, I thought you seemed a little more interested than you usually do when I mention one of my teachers."

That much was true. Something in his very soul

perked up at the thought of Amy.

Arms still folded, Quentin shifted his weight from one foot to the other all the while struggling to look stern.

Shayna, ignoring what he'd hoped was a thundercloud on his face, spoke in a rush. "That's when I decided to take it one step further. I tried to come up with some reason to get you two to meet face to face. I knew if my grades suddenly slipped, she *might* call you in for a conference. But I couldn't be totally positive, and I really didn't want to chance hurting my grade-point-average."

That sounded just like his daughter. Shayna, the perfectionist. She couldn't stand the thought of anything less than an A+ in any of her subjects. Quentin couldn't help the sudden smile but just as quickly forced it away. He had to appear stern. It was his only chance against her.

"And it's not like I ever get in trouble at school, so I had to think of some reason for *you* to go to *her*. It was one of those inspired moments." Shayna paused and sighed dramatically, as only a teenage girl could. "I looked across the room, and there was Bradley. I knew you couldn't stand him because of all the trouble from last summer. Then, it just came to me."

Plopping down on the bed, Shayna looked downright pleased with herself.

"I knew if you found out we were working close together on a project, you'd be upset enough to go and see Miss Welsh." She paused long enough to flash him a smile that tugged at his heart. "And it worked."

Yes, it worked. She'd played him like a well-loved guitar. He wasn't sure he liked how easily his daughter seemed to read him. Fathers were supposed to be more authoritative, more revered.

Oh, who was he kidding? He loved the relationship he had with his daughter. But—the depth of Shayna's deception floored him. Should he thank her, or ground her? He wanted to hug her, but he couldn't reward her deceptive behavior.

"You were happy, Dad. You should have seen your face that first day she ate pizza with us. If I didn't know how much you loved me, I could almost have been jealous."

"And when you saw that I enjoyed the afternoon with her, you kept stringing us along?"

Nodding, Shayna looked up at him. Her eyes were wide and innocent and so full of love he almost melted.

Almost. Quentin scrubbed at his face. It was true she had his best interests at heart. And if Mrs. Morgan had kept her mouth shut, none of this would have happened.

No, that was ridiculous. No matter how innocent his daughter looked, she was the one who chose to act. She was just trying to tug at his heartstrings with her adoring look and get him to go easy on her. No way.

"You can't just mess with people's lives. Because of you, Miss Welsh lost out on an opportunity to marry a man who loved her." OK, so it was a stretch. But he had a point to make.

"How?" Shayna looked truly puzzled.

"She was too distracted by you to pay him the proper attention, so he found someone else."

"He wasn't the right guy for her then." Shayna was direct, to the point, and...correct. He just couldn't let her know it. Neither could he let her know about the part of him that was grateful for her not-so-subtle manipulation. The time he'd spent with Amy may not have happened otherwise.

"That's beside the point," he muttered half to himself.

"Well then I don't know what your point is. I didn't mean to do anything wrong. I just wanted you to be happy."

"I am happy, sweetheart. I've always been happy with you."

"I know, Daddy, but you need a wife." *And I need a mother.*

She didn't speak the words, but Quentin could hear them just the same. He sighed deeply. He ached to give his daughter what she needed, but it couldn't always be under her dictates.

"You have to tell Miss Welsh what you've been up to."

"Daddy!" Shayna pulled her mouth into a pout.

"I mean it, sweetheart. You've been unfair to her and she already has trust issues. I don't want to give her any other reason to mistrust me."

"But it's not your fault!"

"I know that. That's why you're going to fix it."

Quentin just stared at his daughter. She stared back.

He knew what he was doing. Shayna would protest the issue all evening if he let her. She had a way of talking around him, twisting him all up so he didn't know what he was saying half the time. If he said nothing, she'd quit arguing and know he was serious.

Finally, shamefaced, she said, "I just wanted to see if the spark was still there." When Quentin still said nothing, she tried one last time. "I think it was."

Silently, Quentin agreed. But he couldn't let Shayna know that. Give her any leeway at all, and she'd be at it again before he realized what had happened.

"Listen, sweetheart." He placed his hand on her shoulder. "I know this is awkward and embarrassing for you, but when we go over to see Rufus, you have to tell her."

Mouth turned down, Shayna nodded and turned away.

Quentin stilled her with a gentle touch to her shoulder.

"What about Bradley? What made him go along with this? He knew exactly how I felt about him."

Shayna looked down at the floor, a blush staining her cheeks.

"He sort of had a little crush on me. Rusty told me about it, and I used what I knew to my advantage." Her gaze stayed glued to the floor, and Quentin knew she was ashamed of her actions.

"How do you feel about him?"

"Oh, Dad, we're just friends."

"Are you?"

She nodded.

"Does Bradley know that?

She swallowed hard, still not looking at Quentin.

"Bradley has feelings for you. I suspect they go a little deeper than a simple crush."

"I know."

"So what are you going to do about it?"

She looked up at him then, her blue eyes filled with anguish. Quentin's heart went out to her and he traced his hand across her cheek.

His little girl. And in such a grown-up situation. She had some hard moments ahead of her, and he had to let her deal with them by herself. This wasn't something he could fix, but he hoped she learned a valuable lesson in how to treat people.

"I— I don't know. I know I'm going to have to pray about it first. I don't want to hurt him."

Quentin nodded. "I'll pray, too, sweetheart."

Shayna threw her arms around him, and as he held his daughter, he'd never felt more proud of the young woman she was growing into.

∂∽✑

"Quentin, Shayna, come in." Amy avoided looking directly at Shayna. She swallowed nervously, not sure how to tell Quentin the latest.

"How's Rufus doing?" Shayna appeared anxious, and Amy ushered her toward the little recovery area in the kitchen.

Shayna hurried over to the duck and carefully scooped him into her arms. Her devotion to Rufus tugged that maternal instinct Amy was only just discovering. Tears burned her eyes and she slapped at them with the back of her hand. She was way too emotional for some reason. No doubt due to all the time she'd been spending with Quentin.

"Are you OK?" Quentin's tone was full of concern, causing her emotions to swell even more.

Sidestepping the question since she really didn't have the answer, Amy nodded toward the living room.

"Can we go in there for a minute? I need to talk to you in private."

Quentin's gaze shifted to Shayna. A disconcerted look passed between father and daughter. To Amy, it seemed as though they'd had some kind of disagreement.

Finally, Quentin nodded. "We'll be right back, Shayna."

Once they were in the living room, Amy looked back at the kitchen. There was no door to separate them. She wasn't sure this was private enough.

"Let's, um, go outside. I really don't want to be overheard."

Quentin followed Amy out the front door and down the steps toward the road.

"Quentin, there's something you need to know. You know I really don't like being involved in this, but I think—no, I *know*—it's way more serious than we ever thought." She lowered her voice and whispered, "Quentin, they were kissing. In the hallway. At school." She tried to stress the seriousness of it to Quentin, but he didn't seem to be bothered in the least. And that was something she so totally did not understand.

そうめ

As they walked along the tree-lined road, Quentin decided to play it cool. He wasn't sure it was a good idea, but Amy's sudden determination that they needed to separate Shayna and Bradley sparked a thought he couldn't help acting upon.

"Why are you just shrugging your shoulders?" Amy sounded miffed, like she couldn't believe he dared not listen to her.

"I guess I've had a change of heart."

"What do you mean?"

"Bradley's not so bad after all. I told you that the other day. He's got all these plans to turn his life around. He's going to be fine. Shayna will be fine, too."

"But Quentin, *you* didn't see him in the hallway with Shayna. *I* did. They looked a little too serious to me."

"Shayna's a smart girl who knows what she wants."

"It doesn't bother you that your daughter was kissing in the school hallway?" She was aghast.

"*We* used to." Quentin raised one eyebrow rakishly. Amy's sudden blush nearly took his breath away.

"Shayna's a lot younger than we were."

"Kids mature faster these days." Quentin couldn't believe he was standing here saying this when it was *his* daughter they were discussing.

Obviously Amy didn't believe it either. "But Bradley is *three* years older than Shayna. What's wrong with you, Quentin?" She grabbed him by the shirt-front and tried to shake him. "A seventeen-year-old boy and a fourteen-year-old girl—"

"Girls mature faster than boys." He wanted to choke on his words. He was carrying this too far. He needed to put a stop to it now and tell Amy the truth even though he sensed he was on the right track with Amy's next words.

"Quentin, they're simply too young to be this involved." She stopped mid-step and grabbed for a branch on a nearby oak tree, as if to steady herself.

"Quentin! You were *right* to have doubts. All those years ago, God really *was* leading you. I don't know what took me so long to realize it."

Pay dirt. But it didn't feel as good as he thought it would.

As she stood there, an excited gleam lit her eyes and the setting sun sparked an amber glow in her hair.

He felt a breeze brush his cheek and he shivered.

From guilt, no doubt.

"Amy, I need to tell you something."

She waved her hand in the air, eager to speak first. "I understand," she said in a rush. "Even if Karen had not told you she was pregnant, you may not have shown up. And you would have been right. We were much too young."

Quentin squirmed under the look of acceptance Amy cast on him. *Tell her!*

"I'm sorry I said I could never trust you."

Oh boy. He hesitated before asking, "Does this mean you trust me now?"

Eyes bright, smile wide, Amy nodded. "More than that, Quentin." She took his hand and pressed it to her lips. "I love you."

She loved him! His heart tripped and blood pounded in his ears. He wanted to hold her close and never let her go.

The love in her eyes, the curve of her mouth...he longed to commit every detail to memory. He watched her for a minute—no, for the space of a heartbeat—and knew that was exactly how fast it would be over once she knew the truth.

Without giving himself another second to think, Quentin pulled her close and tipped her face toward his.

"Do you know how long I've waited to hear you say that?" He brushed his lips against hers.

"Do you know how long I've waited to be able to say it?" She cupped her hand behind his head and deepened the kiss.

When they finally broke apart, he took both of her hands and pressed them tight against his chest. "How long have you known?"

"I think I've always known, but it hit me like a ton of bricks the night Shayna made dinner for us."

"But that was the night—" The night he told her the truth. The night she stormed away from him and said he could never be trusted.

It was clear from the look in her eyes that she'd finally changed her mind. That she was giving him—them—a chance.

A sudden sick feeling stole over him.

As soon as she knew what was up, that Shayna had been playing them and he in turn used it to his advantage to make a point, she'd be out of his life. All because he'd been selfishly deceptive.

Feeling desperate, he tugged at his shirt collar. "Amy, I really need to tell you something."

"In a minute. This is more important. The kids are going to the Point tomorrow and we need to be there. We have to make sure *nothing* happens."

Now. Tell her now.

"Amy?"

"Yes?" Her smile was wide, her eyes bright. She placed her hand in his. His pulse quickened. He couldn't ruin this. He'd enjoy it while he could because it was a sure bet that as soon as she found out he'd deceived her tonight, she'd be out of his life for good.

"Uh—this is nice."

"Yeah."

She smiled.

Quentin gave into that smile, stole a couple more kisses, and helped Amy make plans for tomorrow's trip to Lighthouse Point, all the while feeling like a guy who gets to choose one last meal before the inevitable end.

17

It wasn't a day for picnics and kite flying. Well, the diehards might try to fly their kites. Not Amy. It was downright nasty. A good day to stay home with a cup of hot chocolate and a good book. Instead she'd be traipsing around the old lighthouse park with Quentin, spying on the kids, making sure things didn't get out of hand.

Of course, the thought of handholding and traipsing through bunkers with Quentin had its merits. And they could always have hot chocolate afterward. But those were all added perks. Shayna was the most important. She was the reason they were doing this, but none of that could take away from Amy's new-found happiness.

Forgiveness felt wonderful. It melted the chill around her heart and warmth radiated through her.

She loved Quentin. She'd placed her trust in him yesterday and told him she wanted to start over. Her heart's desire! God had given it to her!

They just had to get Shayna on the right track. Then everything would be perfect.

She opened the door before Quentin could ring the bell, and planted a kiss on his cheek.

"Hey," he said softly. "You ready?" He stayed on the porch.

She nodded, puzzled by his quiet tone and the fact that he didn't attempt to kiss her back.

"Is something wrong with Shayna?"

"No." He didn't meet her eyes. "They've already left though, so we'd better be on our way."

Amy pulled on a heavy white sweater jacket with a hood and stepped through the door, allowing Quentin to pull it shut behind her.

"It's chilly today," she said as she headed toward the rental car he still drove. "Much too nasty for a picnic."

Quentin didn't say anything as he held the door open for her.

What was wrong?

The way he avoided her eyes, his quiet tone, Amy knew something was bothering him. She had a feeling it went beyond Shayna and Bradley, though she couldn't say why. It was just a deep-seeded feeling she had. Had she been too exuberant when she greeted him? Did he feel pressured?

Uncomfortable, Amy wasn't sure what to do or say. She had been so enthusiastic this morning, so full of hope. Now, she felt a shiver of apprehension. Not good. Was Quentin having regrets already?

He didn't seem to be in any sort of hurry as they drove down the winding highway. It was almost as if he wasn't the least bit concerned about his daughter. The lackadaisical driving was so out of character for Quentin, Amy knew something was definitely wrong. She was terrified it had to do with her.

Was she being paranoid, letting the hurts of the past dim her senses?

No.

She had the strongest feeling she was about to be disappointed once again.

Her stomach knotted and a dark feeling crept over

her like a shadow. Tears burned the backs of her eyes.

Why, Father? Why when we've just found our way back to each other? I've made peace with the past, forgiven Quentin. And now when my heart's desire is within reach, it's about to be snatched away again. I don't understand.

"Amy, are you OK?"

She looked up at the sound of Quentin's voice, surprised to realize she was gripping the handle of her tote bag so tightly her knuckles had turned white.

She relaxed her hand and looked over at Quentin. "I'm fine, really. Just nervous about today, I guess."

He nodded grimly. "Yeah, me, too."

Amy turned from him and stared out the window, still praying and trying to calm her unease. By the time they drove through the gates at the entrance to the lighthouse, Amy felt a sense of peace steal into her soul and push aside her fears. Quentin had said he loved her and she had to trust in him. God had led her to Goose Bay for a purpose, and though it differed from what she thought it was, she wasn't finished yet. But when she was, she felt quite certain the Lord had good things in store for her. And Quentin and Shayna were a part of it. She knew it in her heart now. No matter what today held, no matter his mood, she and Quentin were for keeps.

She got out of the car, only a little nervous now. Whatever happened, she was where the Lord wanted her to be.

"There's Bradley's car." Quentin took her hand and they walked toward the bunkers. "There's no one else here yet."

"Only crazy people would come here on a day like this." The wind whipped at her face. "I wonder where they are?"

"Shayna's favorite place is the lighthouse, so why don't we head over there?"

Quentin held tightly to Amy's hand, and it seemed to her as if he were almost afraid to let go. He had to be nervous about where this relationship with Shayna and Bradley was headed. She knew she was.

As they walked through the trees toward the lighthouse, Amy felt seventeen again. She squeezed Quentin's hand, wondering if he felt it too.

He smiled at her and her tension melted away. His smile was genuine. No matter what was bothering him this morning, Amy knew he loved her.

"I'm so glad I found you again," she said.

"Me, too."

They kissed gently then Quentin pulled back. "Amy, promise me..." He shook his head. "Never mind."

"Quentin, what? What's wrong?"

"Nothing," he said. "Forget it."

But Amy couldn't. That unsettled feeling was back with a vengeance.

"I've always loved the smell of these woods in the rain," she said determined not to push him.

"I've always loved being here with you. It was never the same here after you left town."

Again that squeeze of apprehension, but she pushed it away as the lighthouse came in to view.

Old, but well cared for, it was postcard perfect. The historical society made sure of that, with fresh white paint and bright flowers bordering the walkway.

What used to be the light keeper's living quarters was now the historical society's gift shop. Just stepping out of its doorway were Shayna and Bradley.

Amy stopped in her tracks. "What do we do now?

They weren't supposed to see us."

Quentin dropped an arm on her shoulders. "Amy, there's something I have to tell you. Shayna, Bradley, come here." He motioned to the kids and they walked slowly toward her.

Bradley seemed upset, and something about the look in his eyes made Amy suspect Shayna had just broken up with him. As they approached, he appeared to struggle with his emotions. Amy's heart went out to him.

Quentin held his hand out to his daughter. "Shayna and I both have something to tell you."

And odd feeling shivered up her spine and tickled the hair at the nape of her neck. "Quentin, what's going on?"

Amy listened in silence while Shayna told of her deception. She was touched, flattered even, that Shayna considered her worthy of possibly being her stepmother.

That was something she could forgive.

Quentin's actions, however, were a different story. Just last night he'd listened to her say she loved him. He'd listened to her concerns about his daughter, and all the while he knew what Shayna and Bradley had been up to. Yet he'd never said a word. There were no words to describe how foolish Amy felt.

"Amy, I'm so sorry."

"Don't." Furiously, she shoved Quentin's arm from her shoulder. "I don't want to hear it." She turned and ran, her steps automatically carrying her toward the lighthouse tower. She didn't even realize her destination until her footsteps rang out on the wrought iron steps that led to the parapet.

Once at the top she stood looking out at the water,

shivering in the cold. The choppiness of the water reflected the storm in her soul. When soft footsteps sounded behind her Amy didn't turn around. She knew it was Quentin but didn't care. He'd just sliced her heart to ribbons with his lies, and she wasn't about to give him the time of day.

"What would you say if I told you this was all a harebrained idea gone south?"

Quentin came up to stand behind her and she found herself wanting to lean into his warmth. But she didn't. Couldn't. She held herself rigid and remained staring out in the distance. "I wouldn't believe you." But she wanted to. Oh how she wanted to.

"When I found out Shayna lied to you, to us, I wanted to tell you right away. But while we were talking, I had this crazy idea you were about to realize what I'd been trying to tell you about us being too young."

"And I did. So?"

"So—" He faltered. "I thought it might take away some of the hurt of me having had those doubts in the first place. But as soon as you started talking about trusting me, I realized you'd see my silence as lying."

"It was."

"I won't argue with you. But Amy, I knew then that it was over. You're so rigid where lies and trust and forgiveness are concerned."

Rigid? Is that what she was? Quentin didn't give her a chance to think about it, because he was still talking.

"I knew there was nothing I could say at that moment to make you understand. So I said nothing and hoped that somehow, today, we could enjoy ourselves together one last time."

The only time they spent together today was in the car. That certainly didn't count as enjoying themselves.

"You changed your mind, didn't you?" She looked at him in surprise. The implication started the thawing of her heart. "Rather than spending the day deceiving me, you brought me straight here. Right to where Shayna was waiting. So you could tell me together and get it out in the open sooner rather than later. You wanted to end the deception as soon as possible."

Quentin stared at the circular floor. Amy followed his gaze. Through the pattern in the wrought iron, she could see all the way down to the bottom of the lighthouse. Though she couldn't see them clearly, Amy knew Shayna and Bradley were standing below.

"You could have spent the entire day with me, following them around. Yet you didn't. Why?"

"I didn't want to lie to you. I felt sick last night. I ruined things between us, and I didn't want to hurt you any more than I already have. I was awake all night, praying for the right words to tell you. Praying you wouldn't be hurt by all of this."

His motives were pure. He loved her. He'd spent the entire night awake, praying for her. Amy felt the tears burn her eyes.

Tentatively, she stepped toward him. She heard Quentin's sharp intake of breath. She stared straight at him, but he didn't move.

"Amy?" He looked at her uncertainly.

She nodded.

A smile spread across his face and he scooped her into his arms.

"Does this mean you forgive me?"

"What do you think?"

Amy weaved her hands through his hair and

pulled his face toward hers. When their lips met, she heard shouts from below.

"Way to go, Dad!"

"All right, Mr. Mac!"

"Oh, and Dad, does this mean I can call her Amy now?"

Epilogue

The bright July sun beat down on the back yard of the old Kincaid place. Soon to be the Macmillan place, it was decorated with pink and white ribbons and bouquets. White wicker chairs were set up in front of a rose-entwined archway. Every seat was taken.

Mrs. Parsons was there, front and center. Before the ceremony began she told Quentin that Foster missed Rufus so much, she was buying a nearby piece of property so she could get a duck or two. For the cat, of course.

Nick St. James and his daughter, Emily, also sat in the front row, along with Stewart Snyder, Miki, and Bradley. Shayna had let Bradley down easy, and the pair agreed to remain friends, though it appeared to Amy that Bradley hoped to someday persuade Shayna to change her mind. Best of all, though, Bradley was now a member of the church's youth group.

Some of Amy's students from school, and some of Quentin's students from youth group sat in the next row. Russ Miller's family sat in the third row.

The only ones missing were Amy's parents. They were vacationing somewhere in the South of France. They said their reservations were paid for long before Amy called telling them about her engagement. It hurt that they put a vacation before their daughter, but her father had graciously welcomed Quentin to the family and told him he never really thought he was a loser.

When Amy's father said he'd just been a father looking out for his daughter, Quentin laughed and said he totally understood.

Russ stood next to Quentin, humbled that he'd been asked to serve as best man. The depths of Quentin's heart knew no bounds and Amy loved him all the more.

All smiles and the picture of loveliness, Shayna stood up for Amy.

At the front of the archway, between Quentin and Amy, stood the minister. Amy's left hand was outstretched toward Quentin.

"Quentin, please place the ring on Amy's finger and repeat after me."

"I just have to do one thing first." He grinned and winked at Amy. Her heart soared. That smile was hers to look at for the rest of her life.

Quentin reached inside his jacket. When he withdrew his hand, Amy's breath caught in her throat.

"For keeps," he whispered as he fastened the pearl necklace around her throat. "Even if I have to go on my honeymoon in a pink car."

Amy smiled up at him and touched the pearl, happy to have it back where it belonged. She knew this sealed their vow more than a ring ever would. "For keeps."

Thank you for purchasing this White Rose Publishing title. For other inspirational stories, please visit our online bookstore at www.pelicanbookgroup.com.

For questions or more information, contact us at titleadmin@pelicanbookgroup.com.

White Rose Publishing
Where Faith is the Cornerstone of Love™
an imprint of Pelican Ventures Book Group
www.PelicanBookGroup.com

May God's glory shine through
this inspirational work of fiction.

AMDG

www.ingramcontent.com/pod-product-compliance
Lightning Source LLC
Chambersburg PA
CBHW022107240626
47153CB00007B/2273